ALL THAT MY SKIN CAN REMEMBER

A Novel

Kate Rang

LADY PRESS

All That My Skin Can Remember
A Novel

by Kate Rang

Copyright © Kate Rang 2025

ISBN 978-1-77335-149-0

"Oh My Darling, Clementine" originated in 1884 and is credited to Percy Montrose, or Barker Bradford.

"Gloria in Excelsis Deo" traditional Christian hymn, original author unknown. The English carol "Angels We Have Heard on High," including the words "Gloria in Excelsis Deo," was written by James Chadwick, a 19th century Roman Catholic priest and second Bishop of Hexham and Newcastle.

Cover under-art painting by Gustav Klimt
Cover and book design by Maggie Pagratis

Published by Lady Press
2025

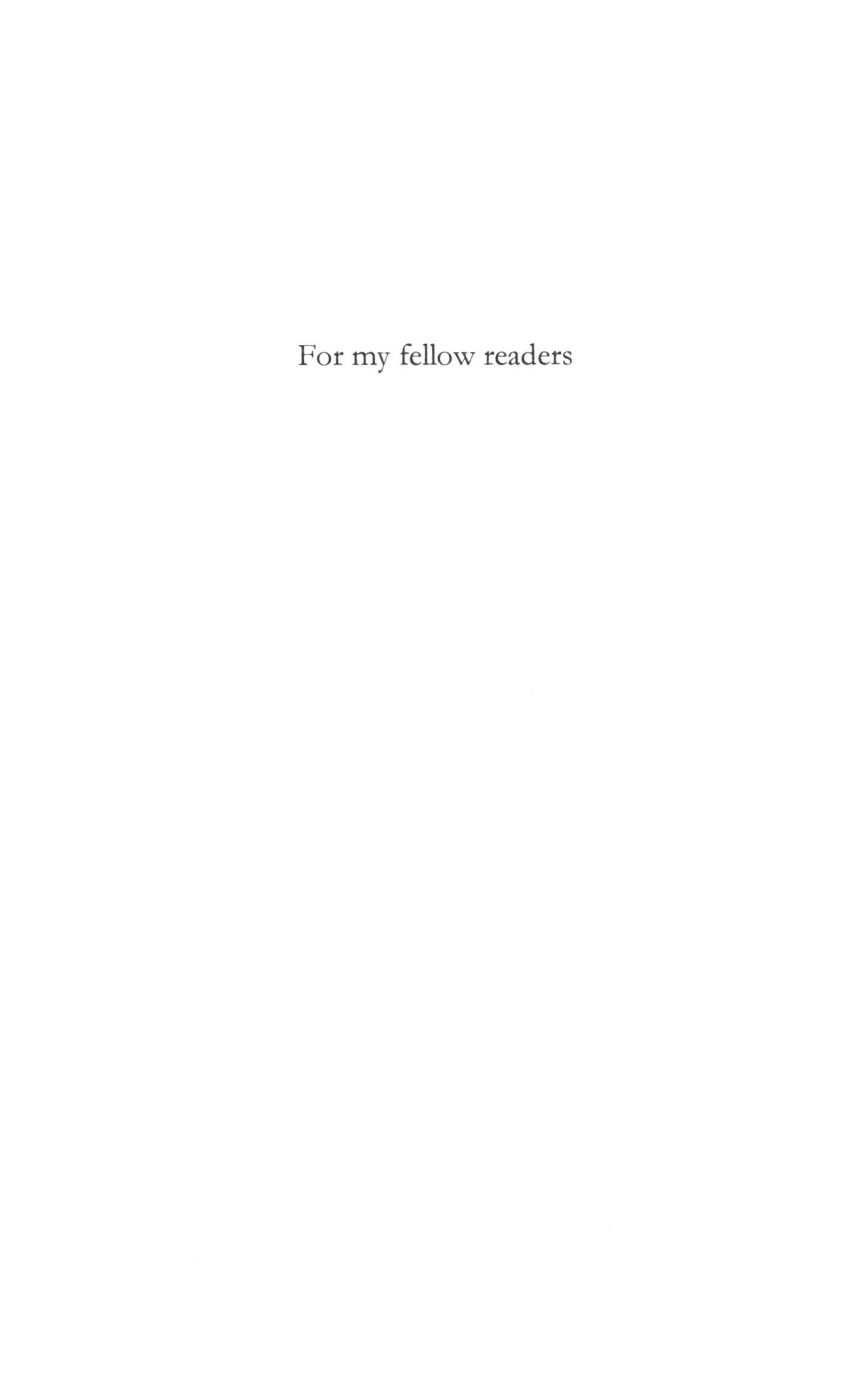

For my fellow readers

Chapter 1

It was good to see them squirm, to feel the power surrounding him and know it was his.

It was a wonder to see the young ones tremble, to look into their eyes and know that they would soon forever be corrected.

With a rifle in his hands, the great motivator, its discipline ready to be cast upon the confused, Samson stood erect and proud. The world was just as it should be. It had taken them a long time, but they had arrived at last.

His eyes glistened with emotion, his hands steady and firm, a euphoric feeling enveloped him. He felt somewhere inside him a symphony, a trumpet, a drum, his heart beating, a maestro he was. He raised the rifle to his shoulder, focused slightly, for taking them out was second nature— and yet still new. Always one at a time as they ran for the woods, where the dangers lay and food was scarce. What did they think they were preserving? The rule of law was the rule of law. It had been decided. For the sake of harmony, love and inclusiveness, each and every one must change their sex at the age of thirteen.

Samson positioned himself again. A squint and a bullet later there was only a mess to clean up. A small one. He was not sure if the males or females caused more of a ruckus. There were studies, but he had not consulted them. A job was a job, and his was done. For the moment.

He watched as the clean-up crew gathered the corpse. It had been female. It should have been male. The correction was likely due any moment.

She had been a runner. Child's play. It was said there was a society of deceivers, those who outwardly accepted the conversion but had somehow evaded the knife, or rather, the laser. In the old days the methods were archaic, and messy, but things had advanced sufficiently so that the whole procedure took less than an hour, with minimal recovery time. You just woke up and it was all gone, replaced with something more beautiful and oh, so new. New was good. A start. A beginning.

Then there were those who sat and stared. The starers, the runners, the deceivers, the jumpers. There was a remedy for each and every one. There was no escaping the new world order, where sex at birth did not matter, and everyone was loved.

It began so many years ago when society ostracized, beat up, excluded and mocked the correctors. Indeed, they were correcting the mistakes of nature or of the "creator," they used to say, a word no longer understood. But Samson knew it well. His mother had been one of them. "A believer," she called herself. Another word that was obsolete, almost, and abhorred, definitely.

But Samson was getting away with himself. All this thought couldn't be good for him. Why is it, he wondered, he even bothered thinking about all these unmanly things? He was a man. It was so good to be a man.

Alas, time for a break. His replacement was due any moment, and he was thirsty.

He raised his free hand and brushed his chest. The faint scars never caused him a single problem.

The occasional tingle and only rarely did he cup them when he was jogging. He did not know why. Those erroneous things were gone.

Chapter 2

Samson decided not to jog to his quarters. In a previous life, before the operation, he had been a medal winner, came in second. He was only a child then, with budding appendages, hips that were beginning to fill his trousers and push at the seams. He was glad that was over. Why he kept thinking about the past these days was beyond him. But it wasn't only the past. Something was happening to his mind, and it kept straying off path. Off the task. Clean up. That was the task, and the only task.

His quarters were not far, and he enjoyed the outdoor air. Not a single scent of anything female. He liked that. Just pure cleanliness. A stress-free emptiness.

He removed his rifle from his shoulder and placed it gently on his bed, a narrow little thing which easily accommodated his five foot four inches.

He was about to lay down for a much deserved rest when something caught his eye. It was in the corner of a dresser drawer that belonged to the bunkmate across from him. It appeared to be a yellow cloth. What was yellow doing here? He strode over, carefully looking around before leaning forward and easing the snagged drawer open. He pulled the cloth out, sat on the floor, out of view from anyone who might come in. It was sheer, and it had flowers on it. What was this? The shock, the tremors, his heart raced. He froze and didn't know what to do. Should he report it, hide it, throw it away? Samson touched the fabric between his fingers. Something stopped inside him. It was unexplainable. Why was he not moving, getting up, doing something—before he got caught with it? Samson did the unthinkable. He raised the cloth to his nose and sniffed. He bent his face into it, rubbed it against his cheek. The most indescribable feeling. It was soft. He did not remember seeing such a thing before. He grabbed it with both hands and spread it out. It was a dress. A dress for a girl. For who? There were only men in here. Samson took the dress to his bed, opened a small hole in the mattress and pushed it in, a little at a time. It was not visible at all, even without the blanket he pulled over it.

He felt suspended in air as he walked to the shower room. He removed his clothing, noticing the smallest droplet of rust on his blazer which he threw in the bin. It felt good to be getting clean.

Samson put on a new suit, brushed his hair forty times till it gleamed and decided to forego his afternoon nap. He was in the mood for a drink. A real drink. Something to knock some sense into him.

The bar was like any run of the mill bar. No lights, or colors or women. Only the corrected. It was lovely, and he felt in place, like he belonged. A strange odor permeated the room, one he could hardly remember, and yet he recognized it. It was the smell of skin, something unusual in it despite the daily blockers. The hormone inhibitors to get rid of those horrid unwanted fumes, like parasites in your body.

Samson leaned back into the chair, his legs spread slightly open, as per a man. For he was a man. He tilted his head sideways. He studied the room. Nothing too unusual. Perhaps the guy in the corner was too overbearded. Did they tweak his drugs? Did they increase his dose for some reason? That was some bush. Samson's own was just feathering, very light, and his upper lip was but a whisker.

He could not stop staring at the man in the corner by the pool table. The pool table. That was what men did. They liked to play pool. The man looked at Samson and turned quickly away.

Samson got up, as any daring man would, and walked right up to him.

"Hey, what's up?"

"Good and you?"

"My name's Samson. Wanna play?"

"Bryce. Sure."

Bryce picked out a pool stick for himself and one for him. An odd move if ever there was one, thought Samson. But he liked it and didn't know why. Had they altered his meds? Had someone tampered with them?

Bryce prepared the balls in a triangle, and bent over the table to take the first shot. Samson was not even sure of the rules of the game, but he was learning. It was difficult finding any pastime which kept his interest long. Only jogging, and that was causing phantom memories, forbidden thoughts.

Bryce positioned his cue stick and fired. It seemed as if he had done it a thousand times. Three balls went in.

His turn. He stretched over the table, balanced his stick, though his hands were not steady as Bryce's had been. Leaning low, Samson got a whiff of something he could not place. An odd scent that was disorienting him. He glanced at Bryce's hand on the table. It was bulky, and there was wiry hair above the knuckles, like a wolf. He didn't have hair on his own hands and he had been taking the hormones for four years now. He looked up at Bryce and saw a bulge protruding from his neck, like he had swallowed a bone. He saw confidence in Bryce's eyes, or was it mockery?

Samson slowly, quietly put down the stick on the table with one hand and with the other reached for the gun at his back. With lightning speed he aimed up at Bryce's face and pulled the trigger. Blood was everywhere. The brain fell in morsels on the table and Bryce was no more. There was yelling in the background, the banging of chairs, a few were jumping on the tables, and as if from a far off distance, he could hear clapping. Someone came closer, and a second, and a third. They pulled down Bryce's pants and yelled, "An authentic! It's an authentic!"

There was a hush suddenly with a few oohs and aahs. What was an authentic? He had heard stories, whispers, like a myth, of those who were exactly as they were born, parading among them, as if they had a right to.

Samson's heart was pulsing fast, bits of brain and blood in his hair, his cheek, all over his shirt. Why was his heart racing? He had killed many times before. But never this close. Never while he could smell someone. Their humanity.

Theo appeared next to him with a knife. "You do the honors." Samson felt as if he would be sick.

"You go ahead. I need to clean up."

There was a cheer in the room as Theo sliced off the offending part. Tyler grabbed it from him, cheering, spit flying off his face. His teeth jagged and feral. The eyes were those of a crazy person. An angry person. An inhuman.

Tyler took his dagger and pinned the forbidden piece of meat on the wall. Samson had never seen one before. It was real. The real thing. Like a salamander on the wall with a knife through it. A fly buzzed nearby and landed on its tail. Or was it a ladybug?

Chapter 3

SAMSON MADE HIS EXCUSES, a shower was badly needed, and went in the direction of his quarters. His head was pounding. His felt his stomach turning and his ears ringing. What was going on with him? Did he feel something akin to pain? That was forbidden; he knew that. Only joy was allowed. Joy for a job well done. And he had done his job.

He ran the rest of the way, his hands on his chest, a drop of something coming out of his left eye. It mixed with the blood and brain matter on his cheek. It felt almost like a scar.

Samson saw the shower door was open, which meant no one was inside. Everyone closed the door. Without exception. That way there was zero risk of attraction or hanky panky as they used to call it. Where was he coming up with these words? he wondered.

He removed his clothing and entered the shower. It was hot and steaming and Samson began to sing, softly, so that no one should hear him if they came suddenly.

>"Oh my darling, oh my darling
>Oh my darling, Clementine
>You are gone and lost forever
>Gentle sorry, Clementine"

Samson sank to the floor of the shower, amid the swirling human debris. He put his face in his hands and wept. He did not know why he was crying. There was a lump in his throat and a void in his gut, but no pain, and there was no scar on his stomach so he rarely felt tempted to touch it. The uterus had been pulled out, or, "teased" out via a cushion-vacuum, to protect it from any damage on its way to the proper owner. The true, corrected female. After all, what use had he for it, anyway? As far as he was concerned the less, the better. It was merely weight. He could run more easily without it, no imaginary jiggling inside. What better gift was there but to be rid of it for the unlucky bunch that bled early. Thank goodness he had not been one of them. He had heard the smell was disgusting. And the untidiness. Imagine bleeding every month and having to wear a mattress in your breeches.

Samson was quite fortunate, to be sure. No breasts. No uterus. Just a perfect work of art in the nether region, a man-made, plastic, removable masterpiece that hung unusually low. He did not know what to do with it at times. He attempted to feel pride, a sense of ownership, but often he was shocked. Shocked that it was there at all. Like an intruder, a source of fear. Why on earth he would be afraid of a phallus as pleasing to the eye as his was beyond his comprehension. It had never truly bothered him, or, on the other hand, had he found it useful. It was just there, always there. He had to remove it when doing his daily business, his maintenance, but he never looked at what was underneath. He tried to forget it altogether.

Samson heard shots fired in the distance, which rustled him out of his stupor. He finished showering and got dressed in his finest outfit. He glanced at the bed where the dress was hidden. Would someone notice it gone? Did he have time to look at it? Not today. Duty called. He was going to a parade.

Chapter 4

HE WALKED WITH BIG strides along the street, humming under his breath. It was that wonderful, terrible "Oh my darling" tune again, which increased the bounce of his gait. He had to be careful not to sway or smile. He knew he was being watched. As an intern, a newbie, a freshie, he had not yet acquired his stripes. After ten years he would be known as safe.

Samson heard the drums and laughter and screeching as he approached the parade. The smell of cotton candy and nail polish crawled over his skin. The tang was getting stronger.

Samson felt her before he turned his head. She looked way over six feet tall, had broad shoulders and long legs. Her hips were narrow and her breasts round and high. Was that a shadow he saw on her face, covered with make up? Hormones were amazing these days, but testosterone was like cockroaches. Hard to get rid of completely.

"Hey."

"Cheers," said Samson and tried to speed up his pace. He was in no mood to socialize.

"You got a light?"

"No, sorry, I don't smoke."

"Too bad."

Samson kept walking, and to his annoyance, the lady remained next to him.

"So, you're going to the parade?"

"I've got a partner." A lie, but why was this giant hitting on him? Or was it that? He could no longer read people, or understand their motivations for anything. Something was undoubtedly wrong with his mind, caring about motives…

"Sure. Just heading in the same direction."

"No worries." What big feet you have grandma, thought Samson. He remembered having read Little Red Riding Hood from his mother's stash of contraband. He wondered what had happened to that book when she was collected for the much overdue operation. How she howled. Like it was the end of the world. How could someone be so attached to breasts?

"So what do you like to do when you're not killing people?"

"Excuse me?"

"Just kidding. A lick of humor."

Samson didn't laugh. He still felt confused by his behavior in the shower stall. He could not understand it. Had anyone seen him he would have had a lot of explaining to do. More than explaining. They would have upped his meds and taken him off the job, which required no hesitation and pure masculinity.

"Okay, gotta go," said Samson.

"Catch you later, beautiful."

His breath caught in his throat. His head turned slowly, melodically, and he looked at his unwanted sidekick, saying not a word.

"I'm Tony, by the way. Or Tonia, if you prefer."

"Samson." To his horror, he even said, "Nice to meet you."

Tony took off in the opposite direction, away from the parade. That was an odd walk. It was not a sway, or a bounce, or a glide. Was that a swagger?

Chapter 5

Samson watched the parade, the grotesqueness of it. Penises on sticks and uterus lollipops. Everyone seemed ecstatic and high-pitched. A nervous, mad energy filled the air. Truly, Samson did not know what was wrong with him. His mind was not thinking normally. There was nothing grotesque about it at all. Just beautiful. Everything was fabulous, fair, inclusive, loving. Perhaps he should ease up on the drugs. Would anyone notice? He barely had a wisp of hair on his chin. What was he to do? He did not want to play with fire, that was for sure. He did not want to mock the system. Goodness knew what would happen. The last person who disobeyed hung on a lamp post. Only his skeleton, that is. Some young ones, the enthusiastic type, had gone ahead and spray painted it. A different color for every bone. They even put a wig on the skull and stuffed a lizard in the jaw. How fun, how wonderful to be part of such a world, to find a thrill in everything, pleasure in every moment.

The parade ended and Samson was feeling odder than ever. His thoughts still on that word. Beautiful. Was he beautiful? Still beautiful? He had been once. His hair had been long and shiny, his lips were plush and naturally red, his budding breasts, real, full of life, his skin blemishless like butterbiscuit. At thirteen all skin was. At seventeen he had threads on his upper lip. Little thin hairs like furious veins throbbing with misplacement. It was better, he knew. It was better.

Samson walked slowly to his quarters. It was his turn to feed the group. Six men, like him. He could not get the image of the swagger out of his mind. He decided to try it. It felt weird, as if he was a fraud.

He had none. He guessed it was a talent, or natural. Why did Tony have swagger? Too many thoughts.

Tonight he would cut his dose in half.

Chapter 6

SAMSON SHOWERED AGAIN AND stood naked in front of the mirror, something he rarely did. He wanted to see himself through someone else's eyes. To be more exact he wanted to see what he would look like in Tony's eyes. Would she see a torso? A man? A woman?

Tony. He did not know why he preferred to think of her as Tony rather than Tonia. Come to think of it Tony was a name for girls and boys. She had called him beautiful. Could he be beautiful? He was so confused, but the thought made him happy. The word did something to him.

Enough of that. Samson walked to the dresser and picked out a pair of jeans and a T-Shirt. He wondered if he should look at the dress. He'd better not. He wouldn't be alone soon.

He was off tonight and tomorrow morning. He would bring food for his bunkmates, and after he was going for a brisk walk along the edge. He hoped he wouldn't see any jumpers.

It was pretty outside at this time of day. The sun was starting to set, the sky purple and orange and a slither of pink.

"Hey gorgeous! Hold on!"

It was Tony.

"How come you're out of breath? Don't you run?"

"Not if I can help it. I do weights."

"That's nice. I like to run. You know…"

"Why don't you join me at the gym?"

"No thanks. Not really my thing. You can come running with me if you like. I'm going tomorrow."

"Sure… See you at seven?"

"Sounds good."

He was amazed at his cool. Tony was gorgeous. Her eyes, that is, and her face, and he was even fascinated by her defiant five o'clock shadow. Oh well.

Once along the edge of the cliff, where the self-euthanizers released themselves, Samson decided to do a little jog, very light, when he heard someone singing his private song.

"Dreadful sorry, dreadful sorry, dreadful sorry, Clementine."

He was rattled and glanced furtively around for the source. Nothing. He bent down as if to stretch his legs and caught the outline of a person go over the edge. Not jump. They seemed to have slid down. Disappeared.

He approached for a closer look. What he saw took his breath away. There were trees down below. Everything was covered in foliage and moss, except one wide, evenly planed slab. It looked like a step.

Samson dropped to his knees and onto his stomach. He extended his arm as much as possible to feel if it was natural or manmade. An exceptionally shimmering pebble caught his eye. Were pebbles that round?

The flat rock was too far for him to reach, but one leg extension would do it. He could almost feel his foot on it. *Would I get in trouble if I descended one step?* He doubted it. Besides, no one would think of coming here to look for him. Everyone knew he hated jumpers.

He hesitated. The edge of the cliff was steep, and goodness knew what was down there. It might very well be an empty pit, or a garbage dump full of rats, or wild animals, or even worse, putrid disease. Not to mention the risk of falling. He tilted his head to see the gleaming object better. It could be nothing, an optical illusion, but he was in the mood for more of… beautiful. Tony's boldness was rubbing off on him. He was feeling daring. That had been happening a lot lately.

Still on his stomach, he swiveled his body around, his feet aiming for the step, and he did it. He touched the slab with his shoe, and reached out the other foot, and steadied himself. He crouched and looked around. No humans, nothing unusual, but yes, there was a shiny, round ball cramped between "the step" and another rock. He took a stick and gently eased it out of the wedge. It was smooth and white and had a golden fine rod attached to it with a clip at the end. Was this an earring? It was pretty. Whose was it? Should he take it? He was beginning to be a real klepto. First the dress and now this.

Take it, don't take it? he thought as he slipped the jewel into his pocket. He breathed deeply, exhaled, pulled it out again and put it in his mouth. He rolled it around and touched it with the tip of his tongue. The top part was so smooth. He was becoming stranger by the hour. It couldn't just be the reduction in his meds. Maybe someone was poisoning him. Or doing some kind of experiment with his food. He did not know. He just knew that tomorrow he was going down that cliff, and he was taking Tony with him.

Chapter 7

"HEY, YOU NEVER TOLD me where to meet you. I've been looking all over."

"Yeah, I just assumed you'd come around the last spot we talked. Sorry."

"Whoa, this sure is some place you picked. You mind if we move away from the edge?"

"Actually…"

"What? Go ahead, spit it out."

"Well, I'm craving adventure. Something crazy. Are you up for it?"

"What exactly am I signing up for if I say yes?"

"Be warned, it's completely insane. Almost suicidal."

"Tell me."

"First, are you a talker or the strong silent type? I really don't want to get into trouble, you know. Not even sure if it's forbidden. I mean, it's completely preposterous."

Tony reached out her huge hand and startled him. She gently placed two fingers under Samson's chin. Samson felt as if he would pass out. It was unreal to be touched, unexpected, and it paralyzed him.

"I would never tell on you, beautiful, if that's what you're asking." Tony's voice was deeper than the last time they had spoken, and it had a different cadence. It was low and serious.

"Well, I'm the curious type and want to go see what's down there. Just, you know, why not? They never explicitly said it was forbidden."

"Why would you wanna go down there? That's where people jump to off themselves."

"Come on. Things have been mundane and routine lately. Besides, I could use a pick me up. We'll just go a few steps and come right back up. You can call it treasure hunting." Samson pulled out the earring, held it close to his chest, winked and put it back in his pocket.

Tony was silent for a few seconds, a hard-to-read expression on her face.

"Okay, beautiful Samson."

She sat along the edge of the cliff, her legs dangling and patted the space next to her.

"Don't say that to me again. I know I'm not," he said as he sat beside Tony.

"Oh, but you are. You are blinded, but I can see things you can't. The cut of your chin, the brown of your eyes, the pout of your lips."

Stop, thought Samson, you're killing me. I don't know how much more of this I can take. All this kindness, it was making him soft. And he did not want to be soft. He would not survive his job.

But Samson said not a word in response. He just started to hum, barely audible. "Ruby lips above the water, blowing bubbles soft and fine."

"What was that?"

"Nothing. Not sure where I heard it. It just keeps popping up in my mind."

"By the way, what's your name from before?"

"Excuse me one second," said Samson, wanting to evade the question. Tony sure did say a lot of unordinary things though he couldn't help wanting more, as if he was hungry for them. The words, the strangeness of them, the freedom of them.

"Hold on, where are you going?"

Samson had stretched his leg and was almost touching the slab.

"You'll fall. Those rocks don't look steady."

"Live a little," he said and jumped the rest of the way.

He stood, hands on his hips, and jutted his chin up. "See? It's steady. I'm the queen of the mountain," he said softly so that only Tony could hear. He leaned forward just a bit. "Are you too afraid to join me?"

He turned abruptly and sat on the "step." He slid his bottom off the rock and began to inch his way downwards.

"Buddy, you're going to get us both killed," mumbled Tony as she followed him.

Samson looked back for a quick second and marveled at how easy the descent seemed for Tony with her long muscular legs.

Up ahead there were four narrow trees, lined up side by side. He slid closer, unable to see much with all the jutting rocks and foliage.

And he felt the earth fall from under him. He couldn't yell or shout for help—he was falling too fast. His heart raced, and he flailed his arms.

He tried to bring his legs to his chest and pull his head in but couldn't. He was going down hard. He felt the world turning and nothing more.

He regained consciousness to pressing lips, a mouth on his, blowing air into him. "Come on, wake up. One, two, three." Someone was pushing on his chest.

He coughed and choked, disoriented, and was turned sideways. He felt water dripping on him. "Come on, you can do it, you good girl."

Samson couldn't remember where he was. What was happening to him? Who was calling whom a girl?

He lay on his back and saw Tony over him. She was wet, and the makeup she had packed on was smudged and mostly gone. She looked…male.

Samson reached for his gun, slowly, painfully… It was gone.

"Get away from me." He extended his arm as far as he could, grabbed a rock and threw it at Tony.

To his surprise he got her. On the forehead.

"Now hold on just a second, Samson. Or 'Samara,' I should say."

Samson was completely floored. "How do you know that? How do you know my name from before?"

"I was there, in the operating room. I'm a head nurse. I saw your file."

"You watched? You watched them take my uterus and my breasts?"

"They didn't take your uterus. I switched you."

"What?"

"There was a shift rotation, and I switched you with the person they had done before. When they saw you in the recovery bed, they assumed the operation had already been done. I wrote 'Advanced Endometriosis' in your file, which would explain the one less uterus."

Samson was stunned. "Why would you do that? Why have I not had any of that monthly mess they talk about? It makes no sense."

"The hormone blockers and other drugs have prevented you from menstruating. But I assure you, you are intact. There is nothing I could do about the breasts. Sorry."

A high-pitched whine interrupted this shocking revelation, one Samson still didn't fully believe. It all sounded so crazy. And dangerous. If it was found out they would kill him. And Tony, in the worst possible way. He was not the rightful owner. What business had he to keep a uterus?

"Did you hear that?" said Tony.

"Yes, it sounded like…a child. Or am I imagining things?"

"You are not. Here, give me your hand. Let me help you up."

"No." He tried to get up by himself.

"I can't," he finally said after a few tries. "Something's wrong with my leg."

They heard the sound again.

"We've gotta get outa here. You either let me help you or we get caught and incinerated."

"Fine." He put his hand out to grab Tony's, but he still couldn't get up.

Tony reached over and put her arm underneath Samson's and lifted him up.

"You sure have a lot of strength for a corrected person." He was really enjoying Tony's strong and bulky arm.

"Hmm. That's a story for another time. Right now we have to move."

Samson felt elated. He could not explain why he would be glad to still have his uterus–if it was true. But he felt fuller. Was that the word? Yes…like more. More of a person. More of who he was. This all made no sense at all. Why would he feel happy about having a uterus? He was a man.

Samson stumbled on one foot, Tony carrying most of his hundred and twenty pounds. It was clear Tony could swallow him whole if she wanted to, or kill him. He felt suddenly badly about the blood pouring down the side of Tony's head. Maybe he shouldn't have done that. Why had he done that? And to think, he would have shot her had he had his gun. Oh no, his meds, his pills, his hormone blockers! They were at the Commune.

He looked up and could see a huge wall of rock and above it a dusting of green. It didn't look like he was going back there any time soon.

Tony had carried him into the bush a few yards from the pool by the falls when he heard the sirens, not from the direction of the whining, if it was that at all, but from high up.

Oh Lord, I hope they haven't found the dress, thought Samson. Or had they been discovered missing? It wasn't going to be good when they returned. But how on earth could they go back?

"Stretch it out as much as you can," said Tony, not mentioning the sirens. "I want to see if it's broken or just sprained."

She massaged Samson's leg, touching each bone on his foot and higher up above the knee. Oh, what a feeling. It was pain mixed with something else in the pit of his stomach.

"I don't see anything broken. You probably just tore a muscle or sprained an ankle. I have no X-ray machine so that's the best I can do. Had the fall been from any higher you would have broken both legs, and I would have broken mine too, did I not have one meter on you."

"Tell me the long story you didn't want to tell me before. I want to hear it. Not later. Now."

"Alright. Suit yourself. Now that I know you can't shoot me...." said Tony touching his forehead. "I'm intact. A man. Zero cutting. No laser. No breasts."

"What are those you have on your chest?"

"Nothing. Just silicone." Tony reached behind him and unclipped the contraptions like they were a bra. He pulled them out from under his T-shirt and dangled them in front of Samson.

"I'm going to be sick," Samson said, putting a hand on his stomach.

"Oh, and by the way. I am a he, a total he, all man, real man, and I find you beautiful, Samara."

"Don't you dare. Don't do that. Be respectful."

"Respect is overrated. Love is better. Beauty, feelings, reality, truth. These are better."

"Is that why you saved me? I mean, saved my uterus. The useless one."

"Why say that, Samara?" His voice was gentle, soft . "You may want to have kids one day."

"Kids! That's forbidden for me. I am a man!"

"You are a girl, a lady, a woman."

"In your dreams," she said, trying to contain the deep and primal smile.

"Come on, Samara. Let's try and find a way out of here before we're discovered."

Chapter 8

Samara was feeling dizzy and nauseous. She wasn't sure if it was because she had missed a dose of her blockers or something else. Tony half-carried her deeper into the bush.

"Wait—stop—look." A few feet in front of her was an object mostly buried in the dirt. It looked like plastic. Maybe a water bottle, she thought.

"Put your hands on my back so I can see what it is. I have to let you go." He leaned over, scraped the mud around the object. "It's a baby bottle. For milk."

"A baby bottle. It doesn't look that old. There might be a baby around here somewhere. How is that possible? Could that be the sound we heard?"

"Doesn't matter. We gotta keep moving."

"Give it to me. I'll hold it. We might need it to collect water when we come across some again."

Deeper into the woods they went. The bugs were ferocious and feasted on Samara. Tony remained untouched. Too many things were making no sense today.

"Take this," he said, tearing the sheer outer layer of his silicone breasts which he had put on his back like a knapsack. "Use it like a mask."

"Thanks. Do you mind if we stop for a bit? I'm bushed, and I could really use something to eat and drink."

"Sit here." He pointed to a patch of moss. I'll look around and see if I can find us some protection."

"Don't leave me here, please. Don't lose me."

"I won't."

Samara lay her head down on the grass and looked up at the sky. What a strange day. How beautiful. How full. How scary, she thought, and fell asleep.

"Over here, over here, over here. That one." Someone was grabbing her. What the hell.

"Stop it," she said, getting up with difficulty.

"What is your name?" the lady closest to her said. There were three of them. A child of about ten, and two women. Were they women? She wasn't sure. She no longer knew the meaning of the word.

One minute she was a man and now suddenly she was a woman. Because she still had a uterus? She no longer knew anything.

"I'm Samara. I fell and hurt my foot. I'm just resting. I'll be leaving soon." She didn't know if she should mention Tony. Were they hostile? Were they nice? What were they? Were they cannibals? They sure looked like wild animals. Their hair was unkempt and stiff-looking like straw.

"We are the collectors. We live on the edge between here and there, and we collect."

Samara was horrified. "What do you collect?" She was afraid to hear the answer.

"Bodies, of course. Some live, some dead."

"What do you do with the live and dead bodies?"

"You ask too many questions, dear," said the older woman. "Don't look so worried. Nothing too sinister."

"I'm limping; I can't move from here."

Samara watched as they gathered sticks and set about making her a crutch.

"Here you go, darling," said the younger of the two. "Don't look so alarmed. Nothing bad will happen to you. Just tell us all about it. All about the torture of being chopped up. We love stories of all kinds."

"I wasn't chopped up."

"You weren't? What do you mean?" She looked at Samara's rib cage. "Are your paps hiding?"

"Where are we going?" They had been walking for hours through thick, hard brush.

"Just a little longer, darling," the youngish one said pleasantly as she cut apart the interwoven vines and branches, opening the path wider.

"We're going to see Oz," said the child skipping in place.

Her bad feeling about this was getting bigger with each step. But what choice did she have? Where was Tony, anyway? Didn't he say he would be right back? Where were they taking her? She wished she could run, but where would she go? Running was out of the question with her compromised foot, anyway. Even if she hadn't been injured she wasn't sure she could make the climb up.

"Is it far?" She was tired, and hungry and thirsty. And although the crutch helped she kept bumping her foot into sprigs and rocks. It was hard to keep up.

"Almost there, mademoiselle," said the girl, giggling.

She had no idea what was funny. To Samara it was miserable, all miserable. Except for the fact that she still had her uterus. Besides, they would take it anyway the minute they found out at the Commune. Would she tell them? She had to tell them. Imagine they discovered it on their own. There would be huge consequences.

"Just a bit longer, my darling," she mimicked her mother. Was that her mother? Oldie, her grandmother? She hesitated to ask questions because she didn't want them to ask her any. What was it with all these sweet nothings…my dear …my darling? It was like someone pushing sugar down your throat. A shiver ran up her spine.

They walked for what seemed like forever and came upon an open meadow. First thing she saw was a Ferris wheel. A Ferris wheel! What the… There were numerous cages, forming a big circle.

"Oh my darling, oh my darling, oh my darling, Clementine…" sang the child.

"What...? What is that song? Where did you learn it?" said Samara, her senses on high alert. There sure was a heavy load of creepy here. How did the girl know that song? The same song she herself kept singing, almost involuntarily.

"Everyone knows that song."

She had to get away from this place, fast. Something wasn't right. "Where am I? What is this...town called?"

"This is Facticity," said the younger woman, "and this is where the normies live."

"Effed what?"

The older woman spun around and slapped Samara in the face. "Don't disrespect the normies."

What the... That was crazy. Who were these people? That was violent. Unnecessary. They were unhinged. Holy Lord, where was Tony?!

That's when she saw him. He was in the first cage. The others were empty. He was wearing his underwear. Just underwear. White briefs. And he was sculpted. Full of muscles and tension. He was holding onto the bars, searching around. Boy, did he look angry. Like he was going to burst out of there.

And then he saw her, a flicker of hope in his eyes. You have to free me, they said. How was she going to do that? She was surrounded by three lunatics, and her foot was still hurting. How on earth was she going to get to the elevated cage and open the lock? She assumed there was a lock. He must be cold. Was he cold? It was warm enough now, but what about at night? Would they leave him there in the dark, alone outside?

"Hello, hello!" said a man with outstretched arms. She hadn't seen him approaching, and her heart skipped a beat. She was wired tight. She had to keep her cool.

"Welcome to Facticity! We are so thrilled to have you. You must have gone through so much to get here, I know. But now that you're here it will all be worth it. We preach not, we kill not, and we cut not! And we're joyful!" he said with a grin as big as his stomach.

"Welcome, my dear, welcome, my darling. You are home now." He leaned over to give her a hug.

Samara cringed. Who was this man with obscene indulgence written all over his face touching her?

"Thank you, girls," he said to the collectors, handing them a piece of paper. "I will take it from here."

He put his arms around Samara's shoulders and began walking opposite the cages. She looked back at Tony. This time it was her eyes that said help me.

Chapter 9

"WHY IS THIS PLACE called Facticity?" asked Samara as soon as they were inside what appeared to be this strange man's house. It was either she find her courage or die. She did not trust their overly sweet demeanor. Some kind of deception lay behind it, she was sure.

"Excuse me, my dear, how about we exchange a few pleasantries first? My name is Milder Oswald, and yours?"

"Samara. My friend is in the cage. I'd like him out. We came here separately, but we're together."

"Came? You mean you were brought."

"Kidnapped, practically."

"No matter. Who is your father, Samara?"

"I have no father. I was produced in a uterus that now belongs to its rightful owner. It was previously my mother's. I am one of the few left who was born in a primitive way to a primitive mother. It's barbaric. I actually came out of her vagina. And she used her mamms to feed me. Can you believe that?"

"That is where all humans come from, Samara. Or at least the ones who have no severe health impediment during birth."

"Nonsense. The uterus is removed at thirteen or for the 'surprised' ones as soon as contractions begin and the baby is carefully extracted. Sometimes the uterus is damaged irreparably during the process and must be discarded."

"How do you know this, Samara? How do you know this is true?"

"I know. I've been told. I learned everything at the academy."

"The academy…I understand," he said as if she were a child. He had no idea who he was talking to. He didn't know the things she had done, that she could kill him without a second's hesitation. But it was better to play along. Let him think she was some innocent little girl, a victim. Was she a victim? At this point, she knew nothing. After all, she had thought she had been cleansed of her…what did they call it before…? Womb.

"Why is my friend in a cage? Why were we brought here?"

"I have too many biological offspring, Samara. If I continue it will bring about deformities in the population. It is mostly women who 'jump' so we have very few men, hence the cages for the intact male arrivals. They are scarce. We are trying to recreate a world of normies. Normal people. It's not as easy as it looks. Everyone's been cut up and disfigured. The Commune, where you came from, is of no concern. They will extinguish themselves eventually. Their system of reproduction is not sustainable. Only pleasure as a reward motivates people to copulate. Without sincere parts there is no thrill. More importantly, when you remove the uterus to implant it somewhere else the body rejects it. It rots and falls out. That is why they have come up with a new process, which will also fail."

Samara's mouth dropped. What blasphemy. What was he talking about? How did he know this? Was he manipulating her with lies to go along with whatever scheme he had planned?

"I see doubt in your eyes, Samara. Allow me to continue. Then you can decide for yourself if you want to help us."

"Please do continue," she said, suppressing her anger and trying to regain control of her facial expressions.

"Your city, the Commune, has adopted a new system where they take perfectly good, young uteruses, put them in vitro and reuse them over and over to replenish the population. They even take older, functional ones at times, if the extraction had not occurred for some reason at puberty."

"What!? That's not true! They assign them to the correct owners!"

"False, my dear. You have been lied to. I have spies up there and some have returned with sketches and notes, long hand, of course. We cannot risk cameras and the like."

"This is disgusting. What are you planning to do with Tony?"

"Oh, Tony is a lucky man. He's what? Twenty-two? Twenty-five? He can copulate for years to come. He must produce as many children as I have then stop. One cannot have excessive inbreeding. It results in unnecessary medical complications."

"So, Tony will have to sleep with women without his consent? That's rape."

"It's a job, my dear. We each have a job to do. But first, we must prepare him for gratitude, gratitude for warmth, a woman's bed."

"This is beyond gross and inhuman. Why am I not in a cage?"

"Women are easier to manage, more agreeable. By nature they are not fighters. They cause minimal problems that are easily handled."

Handled. This guy knew nothing about women. She was not easily handled. Had she been she would not even be here. She couldn't believe she was thinking of herself as a woman. She had been a man for years and now suddenly that she was told she had been spared her uterus she was a woman? How weird that was. One part added to the equation and her whole perception changed? She was still trying to figure it out. What exactly made her a woman? What had made her a man before? Had she even been a man, or a woman with missing parts?

"What do we do now? Where do we go from here?" She had to make him believe she was all in for it—in for his insanity, this perverse sense of reality. There was no way she was staying in this rape-infested dystopia.

"First we have to make sure you're completely weaned off your blockers and encourage your hormones to return to normal. From the looks of it you've been on them for years."

"Four," said Samara.

"That would make you seventeen?"

"Eighteen soon."

"Ohh…fabulous!" he said, almost salivating.

"Anyhow, enough talking. We have work to do." He snapped his fingers and two smiley, maiden-looking figures walked into the room.

"Come with us, darling," said the fuller one with the mole on her cheek. "Let's take you for some love."

Love? She thought she would have a heart attack.

"What did you say your name was again?" said Samara, desperately trying to delay. She had no idea what was considered love here.

"My, my, you are a feisty one. You are not intimidated by all that I've told you, and you want to ask my name again? How courageous of you. Sure, it's Oz. As in Oswald. Milder Oswald. And yours is Samara. It rhymes with Sahara, like the desert. Are you like the desert, Samara?"

Holy freak. This guy wouldn't shut up. How was she going to get out of here? How would she save Tony? She couldn't just leave him to be mauled by hundreds of women. How many were there, anyway? Besides, she needed his help, even if her foot healed, which she hoped would happen soon. She hadn't had a chance to rest it. Perhaps they had the athletics light, the upgraded, supersonic, superfast laser healer with infrared. She'd used it at the Commune. But this place seemed oddly backward. Something messed up going on. Presently she had to be nice. Agreeable. It would buy her some time to recover. What a drag on top of everything else. But Samara was used to difficulties. She had, after all, seen her mother dragged away like an animal, and she survived. Look at her. She was fine. Almost whole.

"I'd rather not answer disrespectful and invasive questions, Mr. Oz, if that's okay. At least until we know each other better," she said to soften the blow.

"Well, well, as you wish, my darling. Besides, you are not mine to have, unfortunately. You are not mine to enjoy, to deflower. Have you been delivered, by the way?"

This guy was getting sicker by the minute. Samara just stared. This couldn't be real.

"Oh, never mind, dear. I have little self-control. But off we go!"

The two women who had been waiting patiently on either side of her grabbed her by the elbows, less gently this time.

"Shall we go?"

"One more second, please," she said stepping out of their grasp.

"Of course, sweetie," said the mole owner.

All this sugar-coating was really starting to make her uncomfortable. That random slap she had gotten from grandma collector told her for sure that crazy was just below the surface. Who slaps a practical stranger for nothing? Something reet was going on here. Super reet. That other word that ended in "tarded" was forbidden since the change. One had to be polite, mannered. It was only right.

"Go ahead, dear."

"Please call me anything but that."

"Would you prefer 'slave,' 'possession,' 'slab of meat'?"

"No."

"Then dear, it is! Proceed with your question."

"Are there other towns besides Facticity and the Commune? And after Tony produces the amount of offspring you require what will you do with him?"

"I don't like competition much, but we shall see. Off you go! Time to make you look like a real girl. None of this butch stuff. That just won't do."

And with that he turned his swivel chair around, got up and exited through a red door behind him.

The two plump ladies coiled their arms around Samara and practically carried her out the door.

Chapter 10

THE ROOM WAS BRIGHT, too bright. There were lights of blue, red and purple on the ceiling. To her right was a huge yellow spotlight. Next to that there was a long fluorescent tube. The walls were covered in LEDs with a wire running through them. It was impressive. She'd assumed they were still in the stone ages.

"Have a seat, sweetie," said the one without the mole, pointing to a copper recliner. Wow. Was this going to be fun or painful? She felt guilty about almost enjoying herself. It was all so pretty. And a copper chair!

"Lean back, relax. My name's Cleo, short for Cleopatra," said the moleless one. "This is Cyril."

Cleo took a pair of small pliers from a tray and started to pull out her eyebrow hairs. Samara winced. This was torture. She could handle big pain, but this was something else altogether. They plucked her eyebrows, massaged her face, waxed the whiskers above her lip and the bristles on her chin. They shaved her legs from top to bottom and threw the plastic phallus into a bin. Finally, they gave her a towel and told her to get into a petal-rimmed basin in the corner.

It was steaming hot. The shampoo smelled like mango. Truly, this was amazing, and her guard, in spite of herself, went down. These two ladies seemed wonderful. Then she heard it again.

"Oh my darling, oh my darling, oh my darling, Clementine, we are…"

Samara's eyes snapped alert. The sound was coming out of Cyril. "May I ask where you learned that song?"

"Oh dear, Clementine was Mr. Oz's first wife. She is long gone, but we all still sing that song. It's cute, isn't it?"

Holy…that's the song she herself was singing without even knowing where she learned it. The same one the collectors sang after they captured her. She'd assumed her mother had taught it to her. Wait, her mother did used to sing it! It was all coming back. What in heaven's name was going on? How did that song end anyway? She only knew portions of it.

"Now what have we here?" said Cleo, touching Samara's hair. "Come, let us see what we can do with this until it grows." She took what appeared to be strands of real hair and with skilled fingers attached them to her short crop. "There we go. That should do. Come have a look." She opened a door and pulled out a huge mirror. Samara was taken aback. She was... different.

"Put this on, sweetie," said Cyril, holding a red and white summer dress. "It has a little padding in the chest area and should do the trick."

Samara pulled it over her head and turned again to the mirror. She looked like a clown, in her opinion, and did not feel like herself. A dress? A real dress? She never wore them even before the change. How would she get used to wearing a dress, much less a red-striped one?

"You look like a princess," said Cleo.

"You do, indeed," said Cyril. "There's a meeting tonight by the Ferris wheel at seven. Be sure to be on time. Now run along and explore the town. See and be seen."

"Thanks."

She kind of felt great. And strange. Like she was in someone else's skin, playing a role, which she surely was. They all seemed nice enough, but cages?! Breeding?! Forced mating? Dozens of siblings?!

She walked straight for the cages. Tony was still there. She saw him before he saw her. "Tony!"

He looked drained, his anger subsided. His eyes popped when he saw her. "What are you wearing? Who did that? You've gotta get me out of this cage, Samara, and then we have to bolt. There is something deeply wrong with these people, worse than at the Commune."

"I'm working on it. I'm being nice, hoping they'll trust me enough and I can figure out where they have the keys, who has them."

"That might take forever. See if you can get your hands on a gun. I'll just shoot the lock."

"But they'll hear it and stop us."

"Think of something, think of something…" he said, tapping his temple.

"Are you sure they're all bad? I mean, they have some unusual customs, but overall they've been pretty nice, except for the breeding part."

"Breeding part? What do you mean, Samara? Tell me what you know."

"They plan to rape you."

"Rape me? As in men or women?"

"Women, of course. They don't do men here. At least that's my understanding. They seem pretty wholesome except for the multiple partners and forced copulation and inbreeding."

"Inbreeding?"

"Yes, they need help with their repopulation agenda."

"Repopulation agenda?" Tony's eyes stretched wider.

"There's a meeting this evening, right there," she said, pointing to the Ferris wheel. "Close enough. You can probably hear everything that's going on."

"Try and break me out before tonight. I don't want to know what they're going to say. I want to be gone."

"Okay, I'll go snooping around. Do you need anything? Water? Food?"

"I'm fine. They feed me. How's your foot?"

"Still hurts but getting better, I guess. The crutch helped."

"Who made it? Don't get too chummy, Samara. There is something crazy off about them."

"I won't, sweetie."

"What? You never speak like that?"

"I don't know. I don't even know how that came out of my mouth." She laughed and winked at him.

Chapter 11

SAMARA WENT IN SEARCH of the keys, first to the salon where she had been pampered. She was scared she'd be caught and had no idea what the punishment would be. She didn't even know if she was being watched. Were they the paranoid kind? The trusting kind?

She could hear them as she searched. "Hear ye! Hear ye! Come one, come all! Let us celebrate, let us have fun, let us copulate! Ha ha ha ha! Just kidding, let us love!"

The meeting at the Ferris wheel had started. She'd better hurry. Where else could she check for the keys, or a gun? Maybe a crowbar? She'd take anything.

She went to Oz's house next. She opened his desk drawers. No keys, no gun, no knife. She returned to the salon. She recalled seeing a waxing type spatula, a narrow one. She didn't know if that would work or if it was even hard enough. Then she remembered the metal file they had used on her nails. That was a start.

Samara slid it between the padded parts of her dress. She hoped it would hold. Wait, did the bra-type stuffing have a wire? Samara put her hands underneath the padding and felt for it. It did. Both sides. Later she would give them and the file to Tony. Maybe he could make something to open the lock. But first, she had to go to the meeting, and fast.

"Hear ye, hear ye! Come one, come all. Today we feast, today we forage!"

What? Forage. She thought they'd said meeting. What kind of foraging?

The place was teeming with women, and a few old men holding mini-signs. They each had a number on them. They seemed…giddy. "Where's your card, dear?" said the woman next to her. Her hair was tied up in a bonnet. It had a ribbon underneath, white with flowers. Samara looked at the women around her more closely. They were carrying baskets, woven wicker ones. Some had fruit in them, others flowers. They all wore dresses with petticoats! Petticoats. Holy…it was really time to split.

"Here ye, hear ye! The auction will begin shortly! Take ye your places!"

Auction!? She thought they had said meeting, then feast, now auction!? Samara turned and glanced at Tony who was behind her, one cage to the right. He looked horrified. They began dragging his cage closer. Four ropes were attached to the bars and eight ladies pulled, two at each corner. The cage was wobbling all over the place and didn't look all that solid. There was a three wheeled trolley underneath that appeared to have been made from a wagon. A horse wagon!

"Come one, come all, the boy is here, and will go to the highest bidder first. Following that, the best bids will win, up to one hundred! One hundred lucky ladies will have some fresh seed!"

From the look in Tony's eyes he could hear every word. His face was turning brighter red with every inch the trolley moved forward. He flicked his eyes across the gleaming faces of the women ready to bid. On him. They were all kinds of shapes, and sizes, and all had on their matronly attire. Samara wondered if they always wore that, even indoors. So far everyone looked like they came out of a fairy tale or the boondog prairies. She felt like she had gone into a machine and come out in a different time, forward or backward she wasn't sure. Hadn't Einstein said that the fourth big war would be fought with sticks? Everything was becoming basic.

Oh how she longed for what she knew. Or did she? Was this better or worse? The world had edges, that is all she knew for sure. This was some messed up stuff.

"Here you go," said Mary Poppins next to her, giving her a mini-sign with a star on it.

"Thank you. What does the star mean?"

It means you are young and fresh and of prime breeding age."

Samara almost stopped breathing. Prime breeding age? Did they expect her to breed with Tony?! There was no way she was keeping this thing. She would hold onto it till no one was looking and ditch it.

Chapter 12

TONY'S CAGE WAS NOW smack in the middle of the crowd of women. How many were there? One hundred? Two? She had no idea, but there were a lot. And there were a few old men. How bizarre. They couldn't breed.

"Excuse me," said Samara to a lady who looked like Mary Poppins. "Why are there old men here? I don't mean to be rude or nosy. I just want to further my education."

"Sure, dear. They are here shopping for their daughters who are likely young, shy, and inexperienced in auctions. The virgins in every way."

"The virgins…" Samara thought she would throw up.

"Yes, dear, the undelivered."

Undelivered…she'd heard that word before.

"Once a woman is delivered of her bulb she can choose her own partner, or partners, if there are several available. One at a time, of course. Whoever can produce the fastest results."

"Results…" Samara was numbed in disbelief, her eyes open like vacant hips. Dumb and almost mute, she knew they had to leave this minute.

"Five hundred, do I have five hundred, first dibs for five hundred. Sold!" First dibs went to a woman of about forty whose frame testified to a few childbirths already.

Wow. Tony was going to mate with her? But she was old, as in really old. *Think Samara, think.*

"Second dibs, four fifty. Four fifty, do I have four fifty? Sold!"

It went on and on. Samara stopped listening after a while, irritated, her mind semi-racing for a solution. The rest of her was fighting off the instinct to leave Tony behind and run. But she couldn't do that, could she? They would eat him alive. Could a man even survive that much pokery?

She'd dropped her sign as soon as Mary Poppins turned away. Now she saw someone else holding it. It was a stick of a woman. She looked gaunt, her skin a faded, bluish yellow.

"A baby please, a baby for me," and she raised the little sign up high. It was her sign! She hoped no one realized...

"What is wrong with her?" said Samara to Poppins.

"She's just having trouble getting pregnant, poor dear."

"Are you here for...too?"

"For seed?" She laughed. "Of course, dear. Nothing wrong with that beautiful word. Say it and hear how delicious it sounds."

Samara gulped. "Seed." It was barely a squeak.

Poppins giggled and turned to face the auctioneer.

"Twelve, twelve, do I have twelve?!"

"Twelve!" said Mary Poppins, displaying her sign.

Mary was not ugly, and she looked nice enough. But the thought that she was going to sleep with Tony made Samara feel ill. The idea that all these women were going to jump into bed with him made her head hurt. It was wrong, so wrong. Not that he was hers or anything, but kind of. They were at the very least friends. And he had told her she was beautiful.

Plus he had saved her uterus. She owed him freedom. A chance. Wait, in order to get him to mate, weren't they supposed to let him out of the cage? She had been all-consumed by the auctioneer and the ladies and hadn't even looked at Tony in a while.

The cage was empty. Tony was standing in front of it, with a chain around his neck.

"Excuse me a moment." She pushed her way through the crowd to the front.

She raised her hand. "I have pre-first dibs!"

"Pre-first dibs…" The words traveled around, with everyone repeating them and asking what it was.

"We've never heard of that before, miss," said the man up front.

"Oh, haven't you? Well, until it was inconspicuously removed from my hand, my card showed diamonds. Diamonds are the absolute best, the top. They are pre-first dibs, meaning there is no charge, and I have the very first seed."

"The first seed, oh my," murmured the women all around. They sounded interested rather than angry. Whatever they were putting in their water or food was working. These were an agreeable bunch. Or were they? thought Samara, remembering the random, undeserved slap she received when she first came down.

"Well," said the auctioneer, "what section is that in the reproduction code, again?"

"Section forty-two, fifty-three, nine, eight." She spoke authoritatively. And it appeared, convincingly.

"Very well. Diamonds shall have pre-bids. One, two, three, sold!"

Samara approached Tony who looked at her with the hugest amount of gratitude she had seen in her life. In fact, she didn't think she had ever seen it. But she knew it. Because she'd felt it, as the proud owner of a part still hers. By some freakish luck. Thanks, and you're welcome, she thought and nodded at him.

"Kindly remove the chain," she said to the extra large man standing guard.

"That is impossible, Miss Diamonds. Please forgive me. The noose must remain." He ticked when speaking. What was wrong with him?

Whatever. They had their own problems. How would they run with the metal around Tony's head?

"Very well. Let us proceed to private quarters and get the seeding on its way." She was totally winging it. She had no idea if these were terms they used, but what the heck.

"Happy fornication, and many healthful returns," the guard sprayed from the right side of his mouth, handing her the chain. He tilted forward, curtsied, and departed.

Chapter 13

"Thanks," said Tony. "That was pretty good."

"Shhh… Just look docile."

"Docile it is."

"I have a file and some bra underwire. Not sure it'll be enough to remove the chain, but I can't find anything else."

"It'll take forever. We have to leave at dark. I haven't seen any surveillance. No one standing guard at the perimeter, no cameras. You'd think people want to be here. You look nice, by the way."

"Don't be ridiculous. I look like a bleeding zebra."

"No you don't." His voice was serious and low again, like he had choked on something.

"Glad you like it," she said trying to seem unaffected. This guy really was something. Had they not gotten to him? To his mind, his core? Had they not cajoled the manliness out of him? He sure seemed primitive. Like her mother once was. Only different. Like a man.

She turned toward the salon, the only place she could think of where they would be alone, and the poor guy could use a bath. Maybe she could find him something to wear. He was good to look at with all his ripped muscles and firm behind, but he must feel awful being so exposed.

Almost there they heard a booming voice through a loudspeaker. "The owner of Mrs. Clementine's pearl please proceed to Oz headquarters without delay."

What? The pearl? Her pearl? Ohhfff…she had forgotten about that. That was Oz's wife's? How in the world had that ended up in their hands?

"We gotta run. Now. Not tonight. I am screwed. There," she said, showing him the way she had come with the collectors. "Only we'll go around there, that part, from behind the building. Come."

"I feel like your dog, but sure."

"You have no idea how bad this is. I found his wife's bead and took it. I showed it to you, remember?"

"They're calling for you?"

"Yes. I'd forgotten about it. I probably dropped it. Or they took it when I was taking a bath. Fudge! Okay, bow your head, look submissive, and let's go. Walk slowly."

They reached the edge of the lot where the barn was and went around back.

"Excuse me, dear." It was a matronly lady with a kerchief on her head.

Samara stopped in her tracks.

"Excuse me, dear." There was another one.

"Excuse me, dear." Another.

"Excuse me, dear." They were multiplying. How many were there? They looked to be around fifty…a hundred? And they were increasing by the second.

"Excuse me, dear."

"Excuse me, dear." It sounded like a chorus. A mob. All women with head apparel. All demure and polite. Sickening.

And they were trapped.

"How may I be of service?" said Samara.

"Does this belong to you?" The one closest to her held up the earring.

Should she lie? How could she? They likely found it in her pants pocket. Why hadn't she thrown it away? How could she know it belonged to his dead wife?!

"Yes, I found it on my way here."

"On her way here, on her way here, on her way here," they repeated in unison.

One squeezed between her and Tony, and then another and another. She let go of the chain. Maybe he could make a run for it.

The mob of them surrounded her and like a wave moved her along. Away from Tony.

"Where are we going?" Maybe it was best if she shut up now, she thought. Enough talk. She did not have a good feeling about this.

They led her through Oz's red door and into another building through a lane directly opposite.

It was bright with colorful lighting. Blue and green and blinding white.

"Declothe, girl," said one of the women, showing perfect teeth.

"No."

A group of unforgiving smiles started to approach. "Wait, I'll do it."

She removed her dress. And they saw the scars.

"Ohhh."

"Ohhh."

"Ohhh."

The mumbling, oohing and aahing, the glares, the fear in their eyes. It was the worst. She hated being gaped at, being pitied. This was getting to be a nightmare.

"Please close your eyes, darling," said a clear voice behind her. She could not tell at this point who was who. They were becoming one big body in her mind. One woman, all of them. One womb. Nothing more than a womb. She was beginning to resent her own. This was gross, so gross. All wrong. Women doing this to women? Or was she a man to them now that they saw she had no breasts. She was no longer convinced of anything. The Commune had assigned her as male. That was that. Now these women saw that she was "remodeled," different from what she was before the assignment. She had always been fine with it. Now she wasn't sure. She almost felt ashamed of herself, being gawked at with judgment, and maybe even with disgust. Surely they were revolted.

"May I ask one question please?" said Samara, finding her voice, anger rousing in her. "Who ordered this?"

"I did," came a male voice from the far corner. It was Oz. He had been watching. She was tempted to put her arms over her chest but didn't want to give him the satisfaction. How dare he? How dare he sit there and watch like a pervert? But everything in this place was unnerving, with their pasted-on smiles.

"Oh, hello, sir. I didn't see you sitting there. May I ask why I was brought here and stripped of my clothing?"

"May I ask why I was brought here?" he mimicked. And then he laughed.

"Oh Samara, what were you doing with my late wife's pearl, my dear? What were you doing with my woman's gift? The gift that I gave her before her demise. Her betrayal."

Uuuhh…her betrayal? How did she betray him? She was effed.

"Sorry, sir. I had no idea it was your late wife's. I just found it and picked it up. It was so beautiful and I didn't want to leave it there in the rocks."

"The rocks? Which rocks?"

"High up near the Commune. There was a step, and it was in between that and another rock. I completely forgot about it, until I was summoned here." Summoned, yeah right. Kidnapped is more like it.

"Well, Samara, you must never touch that which is not yours. Especially not an item that belonged to my late wife. And for this I will go lightly on you. You will only get one strike. Three strikes and you will be removed from Facticity."

Removed? Please remove me and quick, she thought. This place was out of this world reet. Holy insane, holy twisted and effed up.

"My apologies, sir. It won't happen again."

"You can be sure of that, my dear." And with that he was off, exiting from a blue door left of him. What was it with all these colors and lights? She was almost starting to miss bland and boring. Then again, she wasn't. Wouldn't normal be nice? Somewhere in between? Some normal human beings, a normal place, normal rules, everyone going about their own business? Living their own life how they wanted without impositions from others?

"Bite on this," said one of the matronlies, giving her a wooden spatula. A wooden spatula?

"Why?"

"Just do it, dear."

Two of the women came on either side of her and held her arms firmly.

"What the hell is going on?"

And then she felt it. The most horrific pain she had felt in her life. And it kept going on and on. She howled and moved and tried to get away, but the ladies' grip was tight. Two others came to their aid when Samara went completely wild, thrashing, kicking, screaming. She smelled the burning flesh and collapsed.

When she came to everyone was gone. She was alone in the room with the hot and dazzling lights, her left shoulder killing her. She could hardly move her arm.

She crawled her way to the chair where Oz had been sitting and eased herself onto it.

Where was the dress? Her clothes? She had to find a way to go back home. She had to get to Tony. Was he still alive? Had they killed him? Did they have him mating with someone else?

Samara saw the dress neatly folded in a basket across the room. She pushed herself up with her right hand and tried to walk. It appeared they'd done nothing to her legs.

She made to put it on, but it was hard with the excruciating pain on the back of her shoulder. What had they done to her, anyway? She felt like she was on fire. She gritted her teeth, raised her arms and pulled it over her head. With the strap stuck to her wound she walked out the door.

She eventually found Tony. Actually, he found her.

"Psst."

He was hiding behind the barn they had meant to escape from. "Are you okay? What did they do to you?"

"Nothing. Let's go. Their worst punishment is kicking me out, so I'm not waiting around for them to do it. I'm going."

"They won't let me leave," said Tony. "I'm invaluable to them."

"To hell with that. If I'm going to be the only living woman in the world so be it, but you're coming with me."

"How, Samara?" He jingled the chain.

"Wait till dark, then I'll come get you. I'll try to find some cutters. Something, I don't know, we'll see."

The last thing she remembered was Tony's open mouth, his frightened eyes, and his outstretched arms.

Chapter 14

WHEN SAMARA REGAINED CONSCIOUSNESS they were under a tree, the sun was shining and on her head was a weight, caressing her softly. It was coarse and comforting.

"Good girl," said Tony. "Good girl, beautiful." How nice it was to have his hand on her head. How good it felt to have human contact. How precious this moment of kindness. She didn't want to interrupt it and kept quiet, until he noticed she was awake.

She felt searing pain on her back, near her left shoulder, but wanted this drop of gentleness just one more minute.

"I didn't see what they did, but they burned me. I felt it. Hurts like heck. What happened?"

"You fainted. And you're branded."

She was too weak to respond violently as she normally would have. She stared at him, waiting for more information.

"It's a woman symbol. The symbol for female. A circle and a plus sign attached to it directly underneath."

"I know it." She felt herself going under.

"Come on, Samara. Come on, beautiful girl. You have to get up. Stay up. You're extremely warm. I think you have a fever. We have to find some water, a lake, so you can cool off."

"I can't move."

"It might be infected. You're burning up. An ocean with its saltwater and iodine would be better than a pond. I would try and put together some kind of gurney, but I don't want to make too much noise."

"Where are we?"

"We're about two hours from the town. It'll be night soon. We need shelter and water. Can you walk? Even a little. I'll help, but with this choker it's slow-going."

The chain was rolled around Tony's neck multiple times. It looked like a snake, and he looked like a prisoner from the dark ages.

"I can walk but for how long I don't know."

"Good girl," he said and helped her up with one hand, the other on the links.

They walked for an hour or so, Samara wobbly, hanging on Tony who was gasping for air and holding the steel away from his Adam's apple.

"Do you think they'll come after us?"

"The Commune or the psychos at Facticity?"

"Both. Either."

"I don't think so. The guard saw me carrying you and turned the other way. I got the impression he wanted us to go, like he was rooting for us or something. And the rest of Facticity, well, they are unadventurous, and most of the citizens of the Commune are content, and afraid of down below."

She hoped he was right and had no strength to argue or debate.

Finally, they found a small cave. Would they both fit?

"You go first," she said.

"No, I need to find something potable. I won't be long. Go inside and rest."

He returned with some leaves. "Here, just take the moisture off these. Tomorrow we'll find water. It's getting dark, and we don't know what's out here."

He went in next to Samara and held her close for warmth. The cold was good for her, but he was suffering only in his underwear.

"Let me go on top of you. You'll die like that."

Tony didn't protest. She lay on him, in her dainty dress, her wounded flesh exposed to the air. The fine straps and the open back helped. This isn't so bad, she thought as she fell asleep.

She woke to Tony's snoring. Wow, that's what an intact man sounded like? That was powerful. And the smell of him was deep and potent, smelled nothing like her own skin. She liked it.

For no reason at all, her face still on his chest, her mouth flattened against him, she put her lips together and kissed his inflated pectoral muscle. There was long stubble where he had shaved, back at the Commune, she guessed, trying to hide that he was male.

Shivers when down her body. Wow, what a pair of lips can do. The very intact part of him grew. She became afraid, but also ignited. Her hips began to move up and down, ever so subtly, allowing her body to decide. She brought her lips still lower on his chest. The feeling of skin against her mouth numbed her mind and made her feel everything new in neglected parts.

Tony grabbed her by the hair, pulled her to him and put his lips on her neck. She thought she would die. Never in her wildest dreams had she imagined a kiss to her neck could send electric jolts up her spine and to her inner thighs. The blockers were wearing off, indeed. Her body was on fire, the fever made the world turn, and yet she wanted… something… needed… something. Tony kissed her again on the neck, a little higher, near her ear. She no longer knew where she was, the world was dancing, she was swaying. She turned her head to the side and rubbed her cheek on his. Up and down, gently she moved, as if her body knew what to do, as if it was made to seduce…this man. She instinctively knew how to drive him crazy. She moved her lips closer to his and grazed just the corner of them with hers. He grabbed her hair tighter and kissed her on the mouth. "Oh, Samara, you are so beautiful," he said and started to move his hips up and down with her. He kissed her neck again, then back up to her lips and behind her ear, and on her ear, back to her neck.

"Samara," he said, barely audible, "we can't."

She ignored him and started moving her body up and down more hungrily, on that perfect, miraculous part that had caused such turmoil. She kept rising and falling, rubbing her pelvic bone, and couldn't stop. She felt herself climbing to the unknown, unknown something, up there, and then she felt the climax and the release. She was utterly numb and tingling. What just happened?

Tony looked into her eyes. "Yes, Samara, it is good."

"What was that? I've never felt it before."

"It's love. It's how the body loves."

"And how about you? Did you feel it as well?"

"I didn't let myself reach that place. Not yet. I want to wait, if you'll have me, till you're eighteen."

Chapter 15

THEY HAD TO GET SOME water. "Come on, little woman," said Tony, helping her up. "I don't think the Oz group will be coming after us, but who knows what dangers are lurking around here, around anywhere, actually. We have to keep moving. Besides, we really need to drink. And I gotta find some clothes. It was hard last night."

Samara was feeling better. The cold from the night before and the warmth from Tony might have helped, or her own body, just fighting for survival. Her shoulder still hurt, but she could walk unaided.

They pushed ahead for what felt like an eternity, both of them weak from dehydration. They finally came across a trickle of water coming down a rock.

Tony let Samara go first then drank himself. "If there's water here, there's surely more nearby, a bigger source."

"Okay," said Samara, "we keep going, but we need to bring some with us. We don't know how long it'll be till we find any again."

The baby bottle had been lost somewhere between being pampered and being branded.

She bent down and picked up a sharp rock. With it she tore the hem of her dress and then cut it again in two. She held the pieces of cloth under the drip until they were soaked and handed one to Tony. "It's better than nothing."

"Thanks. May I?" he said gesturing to her hand.

"Yes."

He put his hand gently in hers. This time not out of need but out of want.

They walked another hour or so until they saw a shack. It was dilapidated and appeared abandoned.

"Let me have a look," said Tony. "I'll be right back."

Samara stayed put and watched him walk. She felt a fluttering in her stomach and a yearning, a desire for more…closeness. That part of her that was dead for so long was coming alive.

"There's a well," said Tony, returning dressed in dusty clothing. "And there are bottles and containers. No people."

"You look sharp," said Samara walking to the back of the house. "How do we know the water's good? Like, not poisoned, not full of bacteria?'

"I'll drink first. Just a sip," said Tony.

"Maybe we could start a fire? And boil it?"

"And we could sterilize your wound. It looks better than yesterday, but it wouldn't hurt to keep it clean."

"Won't a fire attract attention? In case someone is looking for us?"

"Why would they look for us? We've talked about this. We are nothing to them. They will catch more jumpers and replace me. I'm just a seed to them. I don't think we have anything to worry about."

He broke a chair and started a fire with some matches he found inside.

Samara brought a cushion from the porch to lay her head on. "Over here," said Tony, gesturing to the space between his legs. She obliged. How sweet this was. Amid all this trouble, this pain, such beauty. One human, another human. Was this love? He had mentioned the bodies love each other, but what else was there? Was there more? What was that feeling in the pit of her stomach? That rumbling and rolling, that want, that need.

She faced the sky as they waited for the water to boil and felt peaceful, satisfied. Letting her head drop further back she could see the house upside down. There was a person in the window, watching them.

"There's someone there, Tony," she said not moving a muscle.

Tony turned his head and body sharply, forcing Samara to get up.

"Go slowly, Tony. No rash moves." They both turned and looked. It was a boy. A boy of about thirteen. He was gaunt, with wide haunted eyes.

"Holyf… There's a child in there."

They sat and stared at the boy, and he stared at them, not moving a muscle.

"Wave at him," she said.

"He looks spooked. Hey, hi, good to see you, bro! Come over, say hello!"

Samara smiled and waved. She looked about her for a weapon. Just in case. What if the kid was a psycho? What if he wasn't alone?

She saw a leg chair with a pointed edge but didn't reach over to get it. She knew it was there if she needed it.

"Let's turn around," said Tony, "and see if he comes out on his own. There is no way I'm going back in there."

"Thanks for the water!" said Samara toward the house, "and sorry about breaking your chair!"

"He's still not moving," said Tony. "Maybe he doesn't speak our language?"

"How about we get out of here? This place is giving me the creeps."

They collected their newfound things, a blanket, bottles filled with water, and began walking away.

"Maybe we should take him with us," said Samara. "I mean, if he's alone... Let's wait two more minutes."

"Not a chance. If he wants to come he can move his legs and follow."

They heard a tapping, scraping sound behind them and stopped. The footsteps got closer.

Samara and Tony turned around. The boy's eyes were bright blue, and his skin was filthy, ash gray.

"Hey," said Tony.

"Pleased to meet you," said Samara.

The boy grunted.

"Would you like to come along with us?" She gestured to the road ahead.

The boy just looked at them. Was he deaf? Mute? Traumatized?

"Okay, buddy, let's go."

Samara hoped he wasn't going to kill them in their sleep. The populace was becoming increasingly unhinged and without a doubt more dangerous. Or maybe it had always been. She remembered a story her mother had told her about an Abel and a Cain. This was some twisted world. She and Tony were just the new installment.

Chapter 16

"WE NEED TO FIND something to eat. I'm starving."
She heard crumpling behind her and turned around.
The boy was digging in his pocket. He pulled out
rolled up newspaper and tried handing it to Samara.

"I'll take that." There was a dead mouse inside.
"Thanks," Tony said to the boy, putting his hand on
his chest. "He's offering us his catch. It's a start. At
least we know he doesn't want to kill us."

"F-foo."

"So, you speak!" said Samara. "Maybe you can
hunt. I have skills with a rifle and gun but nothing
else."

She found a long thick branch and gave it to him,
touching first her stomach then her mouth. "Food.
Kill."

The boy pulled out a knife from his back pocket
and began to whittle the branch into a spear.

"Holy smokes, what luck. Glad we brought you along." She watched him work. Maybe she could learn something.

"I'm Tony. This is Samara. And you?"

The boy looked up but said nothing.

When his was done, Samara found another two branches, one for her and one for Tony. Copying the boy's method, she started to make her own. Her shoulder still hurt like hell. "I can't," she said, handing one branch to Tony and another to the boy to finish.

The three of them set off with passable spears in their hands. The terrain was rough but green. There had to be a pond or river somewhere. After a few hours of walking Samara recognized it— the sound of rushing water.

"Do you guys hear that?"

The boy took off like a wildling, weapon in hand. Tony ran after him. Samara followed along as fast as she could, keeping them in sight so as not to lose them.

It was a river. A river. Better than a pond or stream or lake. They could follow it. They could find food. Maybe it would lead to the ocean. How wonderful it would be to swim in saltwater.

Tony and the boy were up to their knees when she got there. Oh, please catch something, she thought. This is the longest she had ever been without eating.

Tony caught the first fish. A lucky catch. The boy, the next five.

They roasted them over fire on the edge of the river. Soon it would be night. Could they sleep out here in the open? She felt less scared knowing one of them knew his way around the wild. Tony wasn't too bad himself. He had the advantage of being strong and huge. And she would get to cuddle up with him tonight.

But they were not alone. None of that stuff she had done the last time. She didn't know what had come over her. What was that animal instinct all about, anyway? No one had told her. It felt like life. Life at its peak.

"Goodnight," said Samara as she went and stood over Tony.

"Come here, beautiful," he said, patting the space next to him. "Come close to me so I can feel you breathe."

Oh boy, this man was something else. She had never heard words like that. He was a poet, a soul, a living soul. A man. Who knew there was more to being than body parts.

Samara was awakened by loud grunting. She opened her eyes to a bunch of men holding clubs. They looked like the cavemen in books. The noises were coming from the boy. They were holding him, and he didn't look too happy with a rope around his neck.

They bound her next and grabbed Tony's chain and looped cord into it.

What was this world coming to? You couldn't get an ounce of sleep. You couldn't have a moment of reprieve without being attacked. By people. People were the problem, the beauty and the joy. And now this salad in her head. The hormone blockers were all but gone from her system. She could tell. Her mind was different. Her thinking, her reactions.

Normally she would have found a way to attack, but with her foot fragile, her burnt shoulder still raw, the softness provoked by Tony, those new and unusual feelings... Besides which, she was outnumbered and unprepared. There were about ten of them. All male and naked from the waist up. They had round bellies, obviously well fed, and big arms. They were short with beards. Every single one of them.

"Come on, woman," said the one pulling on her to let go of Tony.

"Do as they say, Samara." What was that look in his eye? He didn't seem scared. He was angry. Contained anger. That was the look.

The boy kept grunting and baring his teeth as they were dragged through the forest. He tried to pull away from the man holding him and was hit on the head with a club.

"Don't!" yelled Samara too late. The boy was bleeding. He looked like he was about to kill and feed. Or cry.

After hours of being pushed and dragged and tripped they arrived at a town with signs and posters everywhere. Samara's heart sank when she read:

BE DONE WITH EVE

WOMEN ARE THE DEVIL
BURN THEM
EVIL SPAWN
CORRUPTERS OF MEN
TO HELL WITH THEM
MEN ARE THE RULERS
WE ARE ALPHA MALES
WE DECIDE
WE DON'T NEED THEM

What in the world had they gotten themselves into now? Where on earth were they?

Holy fudgesoli…she was a woman. It didn't sound as if they liked women. Burn them? Like hell. The Commune was starting to look better and better each day. Or not. There was no way she could go back now. She had her uterus, she was off her meds, her plastic contraption was gone, and to top it all off she had a female symbol branded on her back. There was no chance they would let her live. They were not the understanding type. She would be shot on sight. Especially if they had found the yellow dress to boot. Plus, she was an escapee. She could hope they thought she was a jumper, dead and gone. But she had disappeared at the same time as Tony. They would find that suspicious, eventually coming to the conclusion they were together, which would lead them to thinking they had been duped, that one of them was a deceiver, or that they both were.

"Shut up, bitch," said the caveman next to her.

What the— "Sorry." Had she been mumbling to herself? This place was making her batty. One hardship after the next. Or was it the weaning off of the drugs? Hell if she knew.

"Shut up, you whore," he said and smacked her backside of the head.

Fudge, that hurt. She was tempted to end him with her bare fingers, squeeze the life out of him, claw his jugular out. She didn't much like being called a whore. On the one hand it was refreshing being referred to as a female anything, but she was becoming accustomed to it, and its novelty was wearing off. On the other hand she wanted to decapitate this guy.

"Sorry, sir."

"'Ruler' to you, bitch."

How was she going to get used to being called bitch?

She looked over at Tony. He had one caveman on his left and one on his right. Two of them. They were short. He was tall. He was probably evaluating if he could take them.

She waited until he met her stare. Sorry, he said without needing to say it. She saw it in his eyes. I'm going to kill them, hers said.

Chapter 17

THEY BROUGHT HER TO an industrial-type building. A factory. There were a dozen or so women lined up. All attached with rope to one another by the neck.

Some had torn dresses, their breasts exposed, their beaten thighs showing. They had cuts of varying sizes. One's face was black and blue. There was hardly a space of unbruised cheek left. Another had what looked like a bite mark.

"Over here," said the furthest captor, motioning to the end of the line.

He put a chain around her neck and attached her to the woman on her right. But they left her wrists unshackled, which surprised her. Did they think women were so weak, so stupid that they didn't know how to use their hands? That they didn't know how to fight?

True, she was still walking with a limp and feeling weak—the branding, the lack of food, the exhaustion. Okay, she got it. Now was not the time to fight.

Perhaps she was overestimating her abilities. There was no way she could overtake a town of angry men.

They were brought to a large room with tables. The women sat, their chains jingling as they coordinated to cause the least amount of discomfort to the person next to them. She saw sympathy, complacency, and pain in the other women's eyes.

"What are they going to do with us?" she said to the girl next to her.

"Kill us."

"Have we been convicted of something? Have we done something wrong? Tell me anything."

"Please, lady, I just want to eat. I'm tired, and I can barely swallow."

Up close, Samara noticed a raw hickey on her neck. A bunch of them. They were circular and had purple speckles. She could see many similar marks on the other women.

"Who bit you?"

"They took turns."

She thought she was going to be sick. Took turns?! Like eating an animal? Took turns biting a woman!?

"Silence, you bitches!"

What the eff was wrong with these people? Where was Tony? Where was the boy? What were they doing to them?

Food was brought to the table in abundance. There was baked chicken and potatoes and bread and pudding, and juice.

"Some food for the women! Some food for the ladies! Some food for the bitches! Eat up, cows!"

Cows? Samara had never heard such things in her life. I mean, it was imperfect where she came from, with all the involuntary correcting, but surely it was better than this. No one called you a bitch or any animal for that matter. Facticity was a whole other story. Branding? Who brands people? Like animals. She was starting to see a running theme. Animals? We're human animals? Was she an animal?

"You! You! You," said one of the men. He was short, and fat, and bald. He had a festering pimple between his eyes. He was pointing to different women at the table.

Another guard came up and unhooked two women and her, and reattached the chains. She was now free. Could she find a way to escape? Would she even make it to the door? She had to do something.

The three of them were led down a corridor to what looked like cubicles with beds. Oh no, please God, her mother's God, please no. Don't let them touch her.

She was motioned to one of the rooms. It was small, with only a cot and a lamp on a night table. She sat on the thin mattress, thinking. It was the first time she felt calm since she'd stepped off the cliff.

The pudgy man with the zit walked in.

"Hello, I'm Dino. Pleased to meet you, whore." He was more cordial one on one, it seemed.

Samara kept her eyes on his as she started to slowly pull down the straps of her dress. First the left one, then the right.

"Isn't it pretty? Look, I'm a woman. It says so on my back. She turned her body around so he could see the molten flesh just below her shoulder then faced him again, her head tilted sideways. "So pretty, this cow," she said as seductively as she could.

Dino, the cordial, couldn't get his eyes off her chest. "Where are your teats?"

"Gone."

"Gone…" he said as if he had seen a ghost.

"Flat as a board. Do you like my little cuts?" She pouted her lips and stroked the smiley-shaped scars with her finger.

"You're not a woman."

"A blessing at this point."

"You're a Half."

"Would you like some love?" she said, thinking she was onto something. He looked repulsed, which was what she had hoped for.

"No, you're a Half. I won't touch you." He left the room backwards, a mix of terror and amazement on his face.

Her luck was mind-boggling. She was so grateful for her scars, her missing parts, her lack thereof, her less than.

A few minutes later she heard a woman screaming in pain. It was horrific to listen to. Another one started what sounded like growling and yelping. After a while, it stopped. Only whimpering could be heard.

The door opened.

"Get dressed." It was a different man, fat and short as well. Samara pulled her straps over her mutilations, thanking her lucky stars but feeling guilty about the other women having gotten the brunt of it. She was brought to the newly formed line-up in the hallway and reattached to them. They looked ashamed and bewildered. Some stared straight ahead. A few crossed their arms over their breasts, others covered the bruises on their cheeks with their hands and faced the floor. She couldn't see all the injuries they were trying to hide. She caught a glimpse of a big gash on one of them. She wore a cream dress. It had blue dots on it, soiled with red. She was skinny, barely able to stand. Her eyes were lifeless. These women had been eaten. Literally eaten.

Back at the dining tables, Samara looked around for a sharp object. There had to be a weapon of some kind somewhere. But she'd seen only clubs around and that required physical strength. The cavemen were stronger than her.

These people were next-level sick. The cutlery was plastic. Could a plastic knife do damage? How long before it broke and she was punished? She needed to do the job. Finish one off to start, cause chaos then pick off the others.

Chapter 18

THEY HAD BEEN AT this bite-wielding, woman-hating, horror stop for a month. Tony was chainless and wearing a suit these days, the boy too. She saw them from time to time as she raked. That's how she spent most of her day. Once in a while one of the cavemen came to gawk at her, made her lift her shirt so they could confirm what they'd heard. She was called Half now. Half, do this, Half, do that.

Tony passed by the other day. He said hello quickly and moved on. The boy often came, stood at the fence, and watched her. At least he wasn't grunting, not externally, anyway. A boy trapped in a suit and goodness knew what else.

Her eyes followed him, wanting to talk with someone, but what was there to say? Was she beginning to feel like half? Half of a person? She didn't know, but she was glad they left her alone most of the time.

She heard screaming and the cackling of fire from a distance, a pungent, burning smell she wished she couldn't place.

There began to be fewer and fewer women until she saw no more. She was alone, the only woman, except they didn't think she was one.

She regained her strength. The men came and asked her what the symbol meant. She said she didn't know. It had been done to her and she hadn't even seen it, which was true. But she knew what it was. She knew what she was, and she felt her roar growing.

Her foot was fully recovered. She had become strong as before, back at the Commune, and even stronger than that, and the hours spent raking hay, carrying blocks of it, pails and feed to the animals had made her more muscular. The brand on her shoulder healed also. She felt the scab form and then it fell off, piece by piece.

Her hands were callused, her face was burned and each day she looked out for Tony.

What had happened to him? What had they done to him for him to forget her? She remembered his words. How beautiful, he'd said. About her. Isn't that what he'd said? It felt like a different world.

She stood with her rake one day, looking out, catching her breath when the boy came by.

"Rake."

"Oh," said Samara, "that's wonderful. You spoke."

"Rake," said the boy again, but this time tapped his chest with his palm. "M—"

"Oh, you're Rake! What a great name."

"Man."

"Yes, you're a man."

What was he trying to tell her? Had they done something to him? Brainwashed him? She didn't know his thoughts from before they came here and she had no way of surmising what they were.

Samara went closer. Only a metal fence separated them. He smelled clean, and his hair was somewhat tidy. His skin was no longer gray, his eyes a vibrant blue. The bluest eyes she'd ever seen.

"I'm a woman," she said, tapping her chest.

"No."

"Yes. Like your mama. The woman who gave birth to you. Woman."

"Mama?"

"Yes, like your mama. Woman good. Women are good, Rake."

"Good."

"That's between you and me, you understand? Secret."

She put an index finger up to her lips. "Shhh. Okay? You can't tell anyone. It's a secret."

"Secr. Wom goo…"

"Yes, Rake. Women are good."

She reached over and touched his hand. He jumped. "It's okay. We're friends. You are my friend, correct?"

"Fre."

"Please, friend, I need a pen and paper. Will you get me some?"

Samara continued with her chores as she waited for Rake to return. She hoped she hadn't put him at risk. They might have pen and paper here. They had markers, obviously, based on the signs all over the place. Maybe they just knew how to write those words. They were clearly not too bright. They thought they didn't need women. They were digging their own grave, slowly, with each person that died of illness, of old age, of accidents, of murder. And they seemed to be ripe with death here. The biting was just a prelude, it seemed, if the ghastly burning smell was anything to go by. But did they kill their own kind? She hoped they did. The fewer the better. She was biding her time, trying to find a solution that did not include being eaten alive.

She missed her own quarters, her peaceful clean life. Sure, there was a down side. A huge one, and it involved taken parts.

Rake returned about an hour later. He had with him a huge creature that looked well over six feet tall, taller than Tony.

They both stood and waited for Samara, looking at her as she wrapped up her last bushel of hay. She was deliberately delaying going over there. She had become overly cautious. Who was this person? Why did he bring him…her…? She had no idea.

"Half," she introduced herself.

"Sammm…." Rake started to correct her, looking confused.

"But you can call me Sam," she said, giving Rake a look. She wondered what had happened to his brain. Was he born this way? Was it just a result of underdevelopment? How long had he been alone in that house? What had he seen? She wished he could talk more.

"Imogene. But you can call me Gene," said the giant in front of her, extending a hand.

A hand? Holy, this was a friendly person.

"Woman," said Rake.

Gene didn't speak but looked expectantly at her.

Samara was thinking fast, gauging whether to trust this stranger. But her options were few.

"Woman," he said again, pointing to her.

Holyyfff… he just gave her away.

"Well…some say I look like a woman at times…" she said, shrugging.

"Mama."

This guy was going to be the end of her.

"Rake told me you needed help, that you wanted a pen and paper and to get out of here. Is that true?"

Okay, she was busted.

"How exactly did he tell you that? He hardly speaks."

"He signs well enough, and I happen to be fluent. Both his parents were deaf, and he never needed to talk, but his faculties work just fine. While, you're trying to decide if I'm friendly or hostile, let's get down to business. I'm leaving on a cargo trip in two days. Rake says you'd like to come along, leave this place."

Deaf…wow, thought Samara. Was it true?

"Indeed I do, and thank you, but I'd like to take a friend along. His name is Tony, a little shorter than you, slim, fit, handsome."

"I see… it sounds like you're describing the General. He's already been accounted for. They are picking him up tomorrow night, at the gate."

"A General?!" she blurted out. How did they have Generals here? They all looked like cavemen, except for Rake and Tony and Imogene.

"Just another word for generic, hon. Some like plain yoghurt."

"May I ask a very delicate question?"

"Sure, go ahead. If you plan to ask if I'm male or female, I'll answer it for you. I'm a hundred percent woman, with all parts intact. But always call me Gene in public if the need arises."

Samara was really starting to like this direct and no nonsense person.

"What do they need Tony for? Where are they taking him?"

"I don't know. I'm not involved."

"Have you asked the General if he wants to go?"

"Don't know a thing more, sorry. I'll arrange a meeting. Toodeloo!" She saluted Samara and turned to leave.

"Wait!" She was dying for human interaction, the company of another woman, maybe.

Imogene turned back to face her. "If you please."

"Why do you want to help me?"

"Rake and I have become…friendly, and he asked me to."

"Friendly!? You're an adult. He's just a boy," she said, disgusted.

"He's nineteen, not even close to being a boy."

Samara was floored. "Well, his mind is young. He has no life experience."

"Says you. Toodeloo!"

So Rake was older than her? He was her height, pretty small for a man of nineteen. He looked and acted like a boy. She, herself, now eighteen, behaved like a woman in her twenties, she thought. She felt it, too.

Her mind was racing. Would Gene help her or turn her in? Would she let Rake leave with her if she could pull it off? They hardly knew each other, but she was fond of him and felt protective towards this man-child wild thing, she didn't know why. And what in the heck was going on with Tony? Maybe if he came by unaccompanied she could get some answers, if he even approached close enough to have a conversation. The suit was the craziest part of all.

There had to be a better place than this. Where would she go? What would she do? This was some seriously mental world. She was no longer sure she could tackle it alone. Why had she even stepped off that cliff? True, there were more procedures awaiting her at the Commune when she turned twenty-five, but that was a long way off.

She had undeniably changed. Where was the cool and collected perfect shot she once was? Where had her decisiveness gone? All this thinking and second-guessing couldn't be good for her.

"Hey, beautiful."

She knew that voice.

"Tony! Where have you been? I've been worried about you. Have they hurt you?"

"I'm getting married. They're sending me down south. They say it's full of traditionals. And since I have no alterations of any kind they can get a huge sum for me. Food, animals, gold."

"Is that why you're wearing a suit? Why the suit?"

"Everyone you see in an outfit like mine is being traded off down South, provided they haven't been damaged in any way. They have wealthy, polite families over there. They want and respect males. They treat them well. The elders desire children and grandchildren. They say the world is dying, and we must replenish it."

So they were going to trade Rake as well? He was wearing a suit.

"You sure have talked a lot. Are you trying to convince yourself it's a good thing, or me?"

"I'm going, Samara. It's the deal of a century. I'm sorry you can't come."

"Yeah, me too." She didn't know what else to say. She was in shock. She had thought that while she was suffering, being the field hand, living within a fence, gawked at, he too had been having a hard time, in some way. She'd made excuses for his lack of contact, his zero attempts to escape with her. Did he not hear the wails, smell the burnings?

"Listen, beautiful—"

"Stop. Please, just go."

"You are beautiful, and I will always appreciate our time together."

Appreciate? What the hell was he talking about? They had shared something, hadn't they?

"Goodbye, Samara."

"One more question before you go, please."

"Shoot."

"How did the Facts capture you? I mean, you're big and you do weights and could easily have overpowered them."

"That's old news, Samara. Why rehash it?"

"Please."

"They said they had food and plenty of good stuff. And I followed them. They said they would come get you."

"You told them where I was?"

"Yes. It didn't turn out the way I'd hoped. Sorry."

"Okay. Thank you."

There was nothing more to say as she watched him turn sharply around and leave, like a soldier.

Chapter 19

IMOGENE LEANED OVER THE fence, looped her hands together and gave Samara a lift out of the enclosure. She took her into the oversized coat, and they went for a stroll, Samara hidden underneath. She walked blindly, deciding to trust, and tried not to trip on her way to the carriage.

"In you go," Gene said, exposing the light and lifting the canvas at the back. "Simple as pie."

It was dark and quiet, and full of produce, ammunition, and guns. She wondered if she could take one unnoticed. She decided against it, not wanting to cause Imogene problems, which would be inevitable if they had been counted.

Here she was again on her way to somewhere, away from here.

"Where to, chickadee?" said Imogene after several miles.

"Don't know yet. Could we please just keep going?"

"Got to drop you off sooner than later, don't want to be discovered with the extra cargo, know what I mean?"

Samara heard tapping amid the stomping of hooves on dirt. Something familiar in it. She'd heard it before. It was the sound of running. Sloppy, scratchy running.

The thumping of hooves and the squeaking of the wheels masked the human strides that were getting louder and further apart. The carriage was ambling along, steadily so as not to unsettle the cargo, which gave the intruder time to catch up.

Samara hoped it was Rake, not some hostile caveman who had noticed she was gone. The beat of human steps was getting closer, disturbing the dirt with carelessness. This was not the sound of a practiced jogger. This was someone running for their life.

Samara left her hiding place between the crate of oranges and the box of bullets and peaked through a miniature hole in the canvas. It was Rake!

She raised the cloth and extended her hand to encourage him to close the final gap. He leaped and grabbed her with one hand, with the other he held onto the curved beam attaching the canvas to the platform of the carriage.

He was strong, and after a second he pulled himself up.

"Good boy," she mouthed and hugged him.

She signaled to her hiding place, should they come across any untoward people. Highway robbers, Imogene had called them. Highway? What highway? she thought. There's no highway. It's all dirt.

"You okay back there, Sam?"

"Yeah, just stretching my legs…cramping a bit."

"Sure honey, go ahead. Did you think about where you want to debark? I'll be at my stop in a half day's ride."

Rake's eyes expanded, and he began rotating his arms.

What? Samara shook her head.

He made a stroking motion again, forward and backward.

Swimming! "You want to go to the ocean?" she whispered and moved her hands like waves.

Rake nodded wildly, his eyes round and determined.

"Say, Imogene, is there an ocean around here somewhere? I sure wouldn't mind seeing one." She smiled at him as he nodded slowly now.

"Well, there is one down south, but you'd have to walk the river path for about ten miles to get there from my last stop. And you have to be off this thing by then. I need to get home to see my Rakey Dake before he misses me too much."

Samara looked at Rake, wondering if he felt as badly as she did. He seemed oblivious.

"I understand, Imogene. Anywhere is fine."

Hours passed, and it got dark again. Rake fell asleep on her shoulder. Poor thing. Goodness knew what he had gone through in his life.

"Here we are," Imogene said at dawn. "Debark and have a swell day! Good luck to you."

"Thank you so much, Imogene. I truly appreciate it."

"Thank Rake! Toodeloo."

Samara got off the carriage and started walking south, towards the river. Rake would sneak off just before the town and return to meet her. All this was negotiated with hand signals. She hoped they were enough.

Samara walked at a lazy pace, listening for footsteps, human activity, the sound of the river. It was nice being…free. Was she free? She felt free.

Finally she heard it. Water. She saw a tree and sat and waited. She hoped Rake hadn't been caught and he could find his way to her. She didn't want to be alone.

The natural noises around her were therapeutic. She felt strong and healthy. Living outdoors, albeit within the bounds of the fence, had been good for her. She was disappointed, maybe even a little sad about Tony, the way things ended, but it was okay. Had it developed into something bigger she might have been more upset, but who knows.

Samara heard him before she saw him. His running was off, unusual somehow. Did he favor one foot over the other? He dragged the ground, that was for sure. And yet he was fast. Was he running towards freedom or to her?

"Sss…" he said out of breath, standing over her.

Had he gotten taller? He looked bigger. And they had to get rid of that suit. It screamed come and get me.

"S-a-m-a-r-a," she said slowly. "Samara. Look at my mouth when I say it. Ssaammaarra."

"Samm…"

"Yes, good boy, Sammarra."

She held out her hand, and he helped her up.

"Man."

"Oh, you're right, sorry. You're a man."

"Man," he repeated. He looked gloriously happy. He was changing. She herself had changed since she'd left the Commune. She no longer recognized herself. She felt calmer, softer, more resigned. She wasn't sure what the cause was, but despite all the terrible things she'd seen, life was beautiful. She was glad to be alive.

"We have a long way to go. Do you know your way around, Rake man?"

He smiled broadly. "Yyy…"

"Yes, you do. That's good. That makes one of us."

He led her down a hillock of trees, and lower and lower they went. He grabbed her hand at one point, to stop her fall, and he didn't let go. His grip was careful but firm. He wasn't planning on letting go it seemed. She liked it. She and her friend. A friend. She hadn't had one before.

"It's beautiful," she said, pointing out what seemed like a groove between rocks.

"Gg…"

"Yes, we can go. Is that the right way? I don't want any stones falling on us? Besides, we're going to the ocean, right?"

He nodded enthusiastically.

"We need water, Rake. We have to get there soon."

He held up his free hand.

"Your palm? What is wrong with your palm?"

He shook his head. He took her hand with both of his and touched her fingers, one at a time.

"Five! Five miles? You can count, Rake! I didn't know you could count."

He shrugged and looked ahead.

"Smart man! Let's go."

He put his hand in hers again and made subtle back and forth swings.

Oh, this was something she remembered. Her mother used to do that. It had been so long… She knew that movement. Her body recognized it.

"Oh, my darling, oh my darling, oh my darling, Clementine. We are gone and lost forever, gentle sorry, Clementine."

Rake stopped walking and turned to face her.

"You like that?"

"Yyy…"

"Would you like me to sing it again?"

He nodded in slow motion, looking amazed, watching her.

> "Oh my darling, oh my darling
> Oh my darling, Clementine
> You are lost and gone forever
> Dreadful sorry, Clementine
>
> "In a cavern, in a canyon
> Excavating for a mine
> Dwelt a miner, forty-niner
> And his daughter, Clementine"

"Ppp…"

"Yes, pretty," she said.

He leaned over and kissed her on the cheek. A soft, gentle peck. It was so human that it was earth-shattering. She didn't know how to react, what to say. She just looked at him. It felt like the world had stopped moving, paused all the ugliness and everything putrid and cleaned it with one act. One beautiful, sweet kiss. If anything, he was pure, raw goodness. The innocence of his touch made her want to collapse on the ground and weep. Because all this suffering was worth it.

Rake watched her, his eyes open expectantly.

"Www…"

"Yes, Rake, we shall walk." She pulled herself together, trying not to cry, ignoring the knot in her throat. She felt tender, something rearranging inside of her. This could not be good. How would she survive if she was tender?

They walked in silence for another hour. Rake had let go of her after the kiss but touched her back occasionally to guide her in the right direction. They reached a groove among boulders. It looked like an alley, and she wanted to explore.

Rake grabbed her arm and shook his head when she started in its direction. He put his finger to his mouth.

"No?" she whispered.

He shook his head again and led her along the side of the wall of rocks.

"How do you know your way around, Rake?"

He brought his index finger up to his lips again, grabbed her arm and started running. They jogged in silence till dusk.

"Water. I need water."

He signaled for her to sit on a patch of moss. Surely there was water nearby if there was moss. And the surrounding area was starting to look greener.

He sat next to her, pulled out his knife and worked on making a hole in the ground. She moved the dirt out of the way as he dug.

"Give it to me. I can do it. Rest your hands."

She dug as he lay flat on his back. Her hands were becoming tired, and she was slowing down. "Are you sure there's water here, Rake? The hole is quite deep, and I see nothing."

He took the knife from her, and she resumed pushing away the dirt. Eventually, moist earth appeared, and they worked more vigorously until water filled the hole.

He pulled off his jacket, cut out the inner lining and pushed it onto the muddy water. He pointed to himself, leaned forward and slurped. He motioned to Samara. She was to do the same.

She drank till she felt she would explode.

Darkness fell. Rake lay back, and she leaned on his shoulder, his knife buried in the dirt next to him. He covered them both with his jacket.

She wore pants now, thank goodness, but her legs were still cold, and she shivered. Rake wrapped his legs around her. She wasn't sure what to feel except thankful. Life was strange, and she was grateful for its strangeness. The ugly and the beautiful together, a night of cold and stars, of togetherness and nothingness, of doing the best you could.

"Goodnight, Rake."

"Ggg—"

She kissed him gently on the cheek and didn't look up to see his reaction. She already knew as he stroked her hair. Soon she could hear his soft snoring, until she couldn't anymore.

"Mm…Ssss…" He mumbled in the morning.

Samara opened her eyes with a start. She didn't know where she was. She no longer knew where she would wake up each day.

She felt his arms around her.

"Samara," she said, sitting up.

"Ggg."

"Go? Okay, let's go."

They drank some more water, Rake put his hand in hers, and they walked, sometimes swaying, sometimes humming. When they heard the slightest sound they stopped moving and listened.

"Ww…" Rake said after a few miles. He pointed to the lush foliage ahead.

"We're here? Are we here? Holy moly!"

"Mmm…"

"Yes, moly!" She laughed and almost ran in the direction of the bush.

Rake went before her. He held up his hand, telling her to wait as he looked around. Finally, they descended down a steep hillside. He was right in front of her the whole way.

"It's beautiful," she said as she plunged into the river. Her hair had grown naturally, the extensions gone since the woman-biting place. The smell of it was still in her nostrils. She'd be glad never to see it again. For all she cared they could obliterate themselves into extinction. Without women the world was over. The end. She knew that now. Those cavemen… The disgust filled her stomach. She shook her head. He was watching her.

"Come," she said. "Water. Drink."

Rake started taking off his clothes. First his shirt, then pants. And underwear.

Samara couldn't believe it. This man! He was without a doubt a man. Although he was taller than when she'd first seen him, he wasn't big like Tony. Except that part of him.

It was shocking, and she gulped. She didn't know it could become…like that.

Rake grinned, completely unselfconscious.

He jumped in the water and took her in his arms.

They bounced up and down holding each other. Oh, freedom! At long last!

She felt something unusual in her gut or somewhere even lower. This was a strange body of hers, doing all kinds of things, on its own. She felt a hunger, a slight dizziness. Her thinking was numbed.

Rake splashed her and eyed her wet clothes.

"Mm…"

"What, Rake?"

"Ww—"

"Wet? Yes, I'm wet."

"Ww…" and he showed her how he had removed his shirt.

Samara said nothing, just swallowed. She was tempted to take it all off. Her breathing was not normal. She was wanting, yearning…for something.

Rake came closer. He looked at her face, in her eyes.

"Mmm…" he said as he lifted her wet top slowly over her head. "Mmmm…" He kept looking at her eyes as he unbuckled her belt. "Mmm. Mmm…" the sound deeper now.

He bent down and kissed her stomach and slid her panties below her knees. She raised her leg, and he pulled them off. She breathed heavily.

He pulled her down, naked, and they floated like boats, or dead bodies, on the water.

"I'd better take these to shore before they float away," she said after a while, refreshed and calmed by the beauty of it all, and leaned over in dazed motion to get her clothes.

He grabbed her forearm. "No," he said and pulled her close to him. His body was slippery, muscular, and that huge part of him stiff like a branch.

"Mmm…" he said ravenously and began to move his body against hers.

"Ww…"

"You want me?" Samara breathed out.

"Yes."

"Take."

He put his hands on her softest part and caressed gently. "Yes," he said, widening her stance.

He took his maleness in his hand and guided it to make them one. Very patiently, opening the gates she had thought forever closed. The most forbidden of acts—to make him a part of her. The unbelievable closeness. The intrusion to her body that she welcomed.

He moved purposefully now, beautifully, escalating his desire and hers, until she growled, and he growled. He became rougher, pulled her closer, deeper, a light convulsion, his. And after he held onto her, spent.

Her need had not subsided, there was still more to be had, she knew it. She took his hand and led it to that tender place, the warm place of unexplored depth, the discovery of travel…to somewhere. The mystery of her…womanhood. Her hunger. For him.

He pulled his hand away and bent his face into her until she reached, higher and higher, and shook, as in a dream.

"Where did you learn that?" she finally said when she retrieved her clothes, stuck on some rocks.

They were sitting to dry themselves on the edge of the river.

"Ttt—"

"Toodeloo?! Toodeloo taught you?" Samara laughed.

He gave her a sideways glance, oozing testosterone. Full of gentle contradictions, her unquestionable man.

"Imogene...she's been helpful all around." Samara leaned back, content, onto her elbows to take in the sun more.

Rake chuckled.

"Gg—"

"We have to do something about that speech, Rake. Seriously. I want to be able to communicate with you. You think we can do that? Is it okay if I teach you?"

"Yes."

"Oki, doke. Now what is it you were saying?"

"Ggg—"

"We have to go? Look at my mouth. Say 'go.'"

"Go now."

Chapter 20

"WHERE ARE THE PEOPLE, Rake? We haven't seen or heard a single person since we left caveman city. Not a soul in sight. Not one manmade sound. It's too quiet."

Rake looked at her, shrugged, and kept moving his eyes around, attuned to possible dangers.

"How much longer? I'm getting tired, and I'm starving."

"Bii...bit."

She had been teaching him to fully pronounce the words while they walked, but they had to be quiet, just in case, so it was slow going. Still, there had been progress. He had amassed a few phrases. He was a fast learner. She still didn't know if the problem was cognitive or just lack of opportunity and practice. She guessed it was the latter.

"A bit?"

"Yes." He showed her three fingers.

"Three miles or three hours?"

"M—"

"Miles. Got it."

"Miles."

"Hello! Anyone there!?"

They stopped walking and crouched. Rake put his finger up to his mouth.

"Hello?! I heard voices, human sounds! Who's there?!"

"I know that voice," said Samara. "Hello!"

"Over here!"

Was that Tony? It couldn't be. How could it be?

"Tony?"

"Yes!"

"Where are you?"

"Up here! I can see you. Walk twenty steps and look up to the right."

"Why don't you come down here?"

"Okay, give me a sec."

They heard leaves rustling and branches breaking, and Tony appeared before them, jostling down a small cliff.

Rake put his arm around Samara's waist and pulled her to him.

"Hey," said Tony.

Samara and Rake didn't move or respond. Tony was covered in boils. Red, swollen, pus-filled boils.

Rake put his palm up and made a guttural noise of warning.

Samara finally found her voice. "What happened? What is that? What happened to the bride, the marriage, the trade? What on earth is on your skin, Tony?! That's gross."

"Let me explain, please, beautiful."

"Grrrr...." Rake pulled her closer.

"Yeah," said Samara, "maybe you shouldn't call me that…and please, don't take another step. Just tell us what is going on? What is that on you?"

"I was dropped off at a country house down south. When the driver of the carriage saw the sight of the population there he took off. He left me like a pig at a banquet and saved himself. The women were all over me before I could run. And run I did. But it was too late. I have these things on me. I don't know what they are, but I have to find sea water, maybe the salt, iodine, minerals… I've been using leaves and plants until now, eating fish along the way, staying alive."

"I'm sorry to hear that, Tony. You said you caught fish? As in a lot?"

"Yeah. I wove some vine and made a trap. Not too difficult if you know how. I have extra in my bag if you want."

"No thanks, just show us how to do it from scratch, please. Rake can make us pikes but good to know another way."

"Sure." He collected green sapling poles and wove two cone-shaped baskets. He put one inside the other. "That's it."

Rake and Samara each made their own and secured them in the water with pebbles. Tony stayed at a distance but close enough to hear them. Rake's eyes flitted from the baskets to Samara to Tony.

"So, what is this thing you have? You think it's airborne? Obviously it's contagious."

"I don't know. All I know is I expected a bustling town, but there were only a couple of dozen women there, otherwise I wouldn't have been able to run away."

"Have you seen anybody on the way here?"

"No, I have not. You guys are the first ones."

Rake picked a fish out of his trap, took a bite and offered it to her.

"Do you mind if we cook it?"

He made a fire for the two of them, and Tony made his own further down.

"Thanks for the fishing lesson, Tony. Do you have tools, weapons, anything lethal in your bag?"

"I have a knife and some scissors, a towel, a change of clothes. A book or two."

"Good. All those things will come in handy. We're going to the ocean, too. You can lead, just please don't come close."

Samara lay back and Rake put his arm over her.

Tony watched them. He seemed resigned to the fact that she was taken. He was harmless enough, and useful. People could be a resource. It was good to stick together.

"Let's spend the night here and move on in the morning. I'm really tired," Samara said, snuggling into Rake.

She woke to scratching and what sounded like chiseling. Rake was no longer next to her. She opened her eyes and looked around. She dreaded getting up.

Every bone in her body hurt. She didn't know why. Could it be Rake's attentions?

"Good."

Not bad, thought Samara. His speech is improving each day. That was clearly Rake, wherever he was.

She got up and searched to her left and right.

"Rake?"

"Hhe…"

"Where are you?"

"Here."

"Here where?

She followed the scraping sound to a tree higher up behind her.

"Hey there. What are you making?"

He held up a small piece of wood.

"Good-morning," hollered Tony. "Where are you guys?"

Rake got up and flashed a tiny circle made of wood. With the other hand he grabbed her arm and started towards Tony.

"Wait, Rake, not too close. We don't want to get what he has. I'm hoping it's not air-travelling and we don't already have it."

He raised the little hoop and showed it to Tony.

"What is that, buddy?"

"Mm—"

Samara and Tony waited and listened for more of an explanation.

"Sorry, bud. I'm not sure what you're trying to say."

He pointed the object at Tony and at Samara.

"Mma—"

"Show me, sweetie." All this loving sure was making her mushy. Whatever happened to that monster she'd left behind over the cliff? That's how she thought of the person she had been. It couldn't be helped. She'd had no other choice but to kill those people—the imposters, the runners. Had there been another option? She no longer knew. Did she feel badly about it? It was like a splinter she couldn't dig out.

Rake turned towards her and took her hand. He examined the wood and her fingers. He felt each of them. It appeared as if he was evaluating her finger size, and it was starting to dawn on her what it was.

"Rake, is that a ring?"

"Yes."

He took the tiny band and tried it on every finger until he found a fit and pulled it off again.

Samara was dumbstruck. She looked from the object to Rake.

"That's a ring for me? You made it for me?" She felt like someone had kicked her in the chest with kindness. She had never had anyone make something for her, something so touching, so simple yet so big.

Rake pointed the ring at Tony, then quickly at himself and Samara.

"Ohhh, I see… You want me to marry you guys?"

Samara swallowed. Marry? Marry? As in marry?

"Yes, wife," said Rake, dead serious.

"Oh, cool, but you have to ask Samara first, and she has to say yes."

Rake turned to her and looked into her eyes. He held up the ring with two fingers and brought it to her cheek, touched it gently and slid it downwards, gliding it along her neck and arm like a trickling stream until it reached her hand.

"Yes," she said, something stuck in her throat. It was too much, the gesture, the thought, the idea of making it—and the very fact that he wanted her. Her.

Rake put the ring on the ground and stood by Samara, raising his eyebrows at Tony.

"Well, I'm a not a priest. I'm a nurse, but close enough, I guess."

She was starting to think Tony was a nice guy after all, even though he had been a bit of a traitor and selfish and cold when he had the opportunity for a better woman than her and a better life. Maybe this was just human nature…who knew. Come to think of it, maybe he wasn't nice. Or maybe he was both. She was sure of nothing at all. Here she was about to bind to an almost stranger, who happened to be a great lover and had beautiful eyes, and who never once mentioned that she was missing her upper parts. She couldn't even say the word anymore. Maybe one day.

"Do you, Rake, take this woman to be your lawfully wedded wife, to have and to hold, in sickness and in health, till death do you part?"

"Yes."

"Do you, Samara, take Rake as your lawfully wedded husband, to have and to hold, in sickness and in health, till death do you part?"

"Just one second! I want one little thing, in memory of my mother. She said it adds more meaning to everything. I'm not sure what it even means…but she had this tiny construction, a wooden stick with another stick across it, like this." She took one index finger and crossed it with the other.

"That's a cross."

"Yes, I want it." She turned to Rake.

He let go of her hand and went into the bush.

Tony stood at his spot and Samara at hers while Rake carved and cut and scraped.

He returned with a wooden cross made of stripped twigs. He placed it next to the ring on the ground, stood up and faced Tony.

"Thank you," she said, looking at his profile.

Rake nudged his chin higher and claimed her hand.

"Very well. Do you, Samara, take Rake to be your lawfully wedded husband, to have and to hold, in sickness and in health till death do you part?"

There was silence. Rake turned and bore into her with his tanzanite eyes. No pressure, they said. Samara looked back at him. I want the pressure, hers said.

"Yes, I do."

"Please take the ring, Rake, and put in on Samara's finger."

Rake slid it on the second finger of her left hand, the only one it fit.

"We need a ring for Rake."

"Hold on a second." Tony pulled out a thick keychain with a metal ring. "Here, use this." He threw it across to them.

"Where d'you get that?"

"I was a General, remember? All kinds of perks."

"I see," she said, grateful for the man next to her. "Thank you for giving it to us."

The ring was too big, but Rake handed it to her, and she put it on his finger.

"By the power invested in me by nature, by the streams, by the sky and the water—"

"The cross, too," said Samara.

"By the power invested in me, by nature and the streams, and the trees and the sky, and the cross, I now pronounce you husband and wife. You may kiss the bride."

Rake leaned over and caressed her cheek with his own, and carried his lips over to the corner of her mouth, brushed it gently, moved them to its center and kissed it like it was life, like it was his. He grabbed her, picked her up and took her behind the same bushes where he had been carving.

"Hey, guys, can't you do that later? Weren't we supposed to be heading off?"

In five minutes they were out and dusting themselves off.

"Thanks, Tony, for that."

"Th-thankk yyou."

"No problem. You guys good? We can go now? I'm kind of suffering…itching all over."

Chapter 21

"Hey, Tony."

He was up ahead of them, keeping his distance. Occasionally he would stop, jump in the river and get out again. He didn't look too good. His face was swelling up and the blisters were becoming…green.

"What's up? You hungry again?"

"Sure, kinda."

"Rake, my man, you gotta keep your woman fed."

Rake stopped walking and faced her. "Me."

"You want me to tell you if I'm hungry?"

"Yes."

"I could really use something other than fish. It's starting to make me squeamish."

"S-soon."

They walked for another hour. Samara was beginning to feel weak at the knees. She didn't know what was up with her. Was she catching Tony's whatever it was? But she hadn't gone within ten feet of him.

"Look," she said, raising her hand unsteadily.

"Hey, what is that?" said Tony, stopping.

Rake went widely around him and climbed over the edge of the incline.

"Hh…haws."

"What?" She skirted Tony as she made the ascent. Rake held out his hand to help her over. "It's a house alright. Do you guys mind if we go see. I'm crazy tired. Maybe they have some fruit, some greens, milk. Anything. And a bed. Just to catch my breath. We were supposed to have reached the ocean miles ago, and there's nothing around."

"Dange."

"Yeah, okay, but can we risk it? It's three of us, and the reward sure would be good. And I don't hear any noise. Do you?"

"Let me go first," said Tony.

"No," said Rake. "Ug."

"He says you're too ugly with all the sores. You'll scare them…if there's anyone there."

Rake left Samara at the top of the dirt ledge. Tony kept a decent distance from her, which she appreciated.

They watched Rake go inside and out back, knife in hand. He reappeared holding a chicken. He waved them in.

"That's insanely lucky. Do we eat it? Did you check under the floorboards? What if they come back? Is there a bed?"

Rake nodded.

"No," he said to Tony and put up his hand as if to block him.

"What? Not sure I know what you're saying, bro."

"No." He indicated the box-like structure on the side of the house.

"Ohh, okay. You don't want me to go in with you."

"Shed."

"No problem. I'll take the shed if it's empty and not infested with something. Then again, I'll just take it. But, guys, I really gotta find the ocean. I'm not doing well."

"I just need an hour or so of rest, decent rest, on a bed, then we can head off. How far do you think? Could we be lost?"

"Nah, not far now."

"Come," said Rake. "Bed."

They entered the house alone and selected the closest bedroom. She fell asleep almost instantly. She dreamt she was digging her face in a peach. Its juices were running down her navel and Rake was drinking them up.

"Have," she said when she woke.

Rake made love to her like she was the most beautiful woman in the world.

"Do you not mind that I have no breasts?"

"No."

She stroked his wild hair. It had grown again after the close crop they had given him at caveman city.

"I like it," she said.

He kissed her forehead. "Go."

"We have to go?"

"Yes."

They were up and ready in minutes. They shouted for Tony who had made himself comfortable in his new little abode.

"What are you doing with that? We can't take that with us. What if it clucks or chirps? It'll draw attention to us."

"From which people? There are none. We haven't seen a single person or heard a carriage in the gazillion miles we've walked, not before you showed up, not after."

Samara held the chicken tightly under her arm. "It might lay eggs. I want it."

Rake tore three strips from his shirt, tied two of them together and made a long rope. One end he attached loosely around the bird's neck, and the other he gave to Samara.

"Thank you, wonderful man."

"I smell salt in the air. It shouldn't be far now."

Rake took the third strip and tied it to a tree.

"Smmaart," said Tony. "That way we can find our way back if we need to."

It was getting hot and Samara was feeling off-balance somehow. She sat at the edge of the river at intervals to cool off, rose and trudged on. They stopped every couple of hours, caught fish, roasted them on sticks over a fire, snuffed out the flames and continued walking. Still no people.

"I think we're here," said Tony. It's still a ways, but I could swear I smell and hear it.

They ran into a blockage that once might have been a dam, and the river became barely a foot deep. They redirected and pushed on toward the faint sound of slapping waves. The air became thicker, and she could almost taste the glory in her throat as she breathed in.

"You," said Rake to Tony, standing back and placing his hand on Samara's shoulder to stop her.

"Okay, I'll go first."

Tony didn't bother coming back, but they heard him laughing and splashing like a child. By the time they reached him he was on his back, stretched out in the sand. It was white with small pebbles strewn everywhere. The beach went on and on.

Rake and Samara went into the ocean next. When they came out they found a spot several feet from Tony.

"It's nice here," she said. "We should stay. Build a boat, go exploring, catch crabs, maybe look for other people. There has to be some in nearby shores."

"We don't know how high the tide rises, or if it's windy, or if there are storms."

"Look," said Rake.

"Yeah, we can look around first then decide. How do you feel, Tony? How are your boils? Any better?"

"The salt seems to be burning them. They sting. I don't know."

They made a fire on the beach. Rake dove into the water like he had been born there. He came out with a shoe, and a glass bottle and a few shells.

He took off all of his clothes and lay in the sun.

Samara lay next to him but kept her clothes on. Although Tony had already seen her naked on the operating table back at the Commune, she didn't want him to see her now. And she felt self-conscious about her scars. She wondered when that would go away. Would it ever go away?

Chapter 22

"WE NEED SHELTER ASAP," said Samara, getting up after a long stretch. She headed to the back end of the shore where there seemed to be a forest…a jungle? She had no idea, but it was time to find out.

"How about you guys do some fishing, and I'll go exploring, see if I can rummage some building supplies, wood, maybe find a cave or a hut? We can't possibly be the only ones to have come across this beach. There are bottles and shoes."

"No," said Rake.

He came up next to her and put his hand on her shoulder, the branded one. It was no longer raw, but she felt its presence when someone touched her there. She took his hand in hers, kissed and released it. He seemed confused, questioning.

"It hurts over there still, kinda… well… mentally."

Rake nodded.

"See ya!" Samara raised her hand in salute to Tony.

She and Rake walked deeper into the bush. "We need some kind of cover at least, anything, even a cluster of branches where we can make a roof if it rains."

"Want," Rake said, stopping.

He pulled at her. Her breathing slowed, her legs weakened, burning and tingling below her abdomen. She knew he required her, and she needed him.

"Have," she said.

His body brushed hers and with his fingers he pushed the strands away from her face. He moved his hand down her neck, over her shoulder, along her torso and onto her buttock, and grabbed it.

"Nice."

"Yes. Yours."

His gentleness was replaced with savagery, a man famished and determined. He had her like there was no other choice.

They lay together looking up at the leaves and at the sky in between. The clouds were feathered at the very bottom. If there was a God, like her mother told her, boy, was He creative. He must be beautiful to make all this beauty. He must be good to give her all this. This. What was it? Love? Lust? Desire, a gift to the living. The need to affirm life by binding, mating, connecting, creating something out of nothing, out of pure thin air, just energy between two people.

She no longer recognized who she had been. This person she was now was so much more. Her head was spinning, and she felt she wanted him again, something insatiable inside her for his humanity, his maleness.

"Ready go?"

"Not bad, Rake. Your words are coming along. Were you not around people before us, before seeing me and Tony? What happened?"

"Dead. Speak bit."

"They spoke a little? Your parents? They died when you were a child?"

"Five. Think."

"And you raised yourself?"

"Yes."

"Hmm…I had read you lose the ability to speak if you stay silent too long. Is that what happened to you?"

He raised one shoulder.

They walked further into the woods.

"Wait, we have to know we can find our way back. Can we leave like some kind of trail, so we know exactly where Tony is?"

He took his knife and cut a vertical line into a trunk. He did this for every few trees. It was slow going but not a bad idea given they were in unknown territory.

"Greetings," said a voice behind them.

"Oh, you startled us," she said, flinging her head.

Rake grabbed his knife and held it by his side.

"I come in peace. We come in peace," the man said as several irksome children climbed down from the trees. Their skin was translucent-looking. The veins showed through, blue with fine red streaks.

Samara turned around slowly, watching as more descended. No shoes. They seemed agile on their feet, and their limbs looked…malleable? Strong and flexible, like monkeys.

"We are friendly, harmless, I assure you. Come along children, and say hello," he said, raising his long black umbrella.

Samara and Rake were surrounded. The children did not look well-nourished. There was a grayish tinge to their skin, and their eyes were huge. Maybe it was due to their low weight? Their head was large and their hair unkempt and wild. Rake had looked a bit like them when they'd met him, except for the big head and eyes. Rake was beautiful, albeit small for his age. These creatures looked dead, but were alive.

She took a step back, but they were there too. Behind her.

"Mama," said one, followed by another. Pretty soon all of them were crying, whining, mumbling, "mama."

"Are you by any chance expecting?"

"What?"

"They can sense it, you know. The hormones in your system. They change when you're pregnant."

"What?" Not only could she hardly speak, her brain wasn't even functioning properly. She couldn't process what was happening around her. Here she was back to darkness, when things were just starting to look up. And what were these…"children" around her? What was going on?

"Rake," said her perceptive man, smacking his chest, and diverting attention to himself.

"I'm Samara."

His voice had snapped her out of her stupor. "The beach is beautiful. Have you seen it? The water is amazing," she said, trying to buy them time, get more information. Where was Tony? They could use some help. These were kids alright, but they sure looked unsafe. Something untrustworthy in their eyes. Perhaps she was imagining. They could just be unhealthy, needy, neglected, but she wasn't taking any chances.

"You?" said Rake, pointing to the well-dressed man.

"I'm Niger. Very pleased to meet you."

"Likewise," said Samara.

"Now, will you answer my question? To satisfy my curiosity, of course. These children of mine, well, they have acute sensory abilities, and their sense of smell is superb. What is it they call the pregnancy hormone? Human Chorionic Gonadotropin. Yes, that's it. So, are you pregnant?"

Samara had gotten a hold of herself somewhat. "No, I am not. I took hormone blockers for over four years, and I can't conceive."

Rake squeezed her arm. She didn't know if it meant I am with you, I support you, or, why didn't you tell me?

"Oh my, you're one of those, the nonconceivers. Do you know that for years women just killed babies inside their wombs? Just killed them. Did you know that?" His voice was rising, and he was turning red.

Samara was speechless. What the hell was he talking about?

"They just sucked it out, or cut it out, or burnt it out, who knows? Some of them jumped up and down and used hangers, and liquid cleaners. Did you know?"

"I did not."

"You, you?" said the man shaking his umbrella at Rake. "Did you knoooow?!"

"No. Sorry."

Way to go, Rake. Good to add an apology.

"We're very sorry people did that," Samara followed, hoping it would appease him.

"Wellll…those women were evil. It's deep inside them. It's inherent. Do you know inherent?" His face was becoming redder. Holy…where was Tony? There were too many of them. Although they were mostly children they had sticks now and a menacing look in their eyes. They had to retreat smoothly, peacefully, no harm done.

"Look, sir, we're deeply sorry about those evil women who did evil things, and we're glad it's in the past, and we're glad we're not a part of it, so very grateful. It was good to meet you. Now we must be getting on. We have a group of friends coming to meet us shortly and should there be any pregnant women among them we'll be sure to let you know. Lovely to meet you, children."

She put her hand in Rake's, and they began stepping away, through the crowd and by Mr. Umbrella, and went back the way they came.

"Do not turn around," she said under her breath.

They walked to the last tree Rake had marked and kept going. When they arrived at their spot at the beach Tony was frying fish on a rock over the fire, looking serene, happy even.

"Boils are looking better," he said as they approached.

"Forget the boils. Pack up, and let's go. There's some weird stuff going on there in the bush, and we have to leave, fast."

"You guys looked spooked. What's up? You met someone?"

"No time to talk. We're gone."

"Sure, boss," he said and set about snuffing the flames.

"Stick," said Rake. "Fish, stick."

"Put the fish on a stick?"

"Water, bottle."

"Put ocean water in the bottle we found and take it with us? Genius, man! Genius!"

They were nervous and moved methodically and firmly, as if at any moment they would be attacked.

"Way. Same way."

"He says let's go the same way we came. Make sure no one is following us, though. We don't want them knowing about the cabin."

"Fug, man…" said Tony, impressed. What did you guys see to get you so freaked out? The two wildbirds…the two lovebirds."

"Stop. There's real danger back there. Trust me. I felt it."

After about an hour of walking Samara started to relax. She could feel the tension abate in Rake, too.

"There were at least fifteen kids there, more hidden in the trees, and this dude with an umbrella and a hat, and he had big words and was like, super angry about…women. Women who kill their kids, he said, something like that."

"Kill their kids?"

"Yeah, something about sucking, and hangers, and detergent. I have no clue what he was talking about."

"Detergent? Ahhh…I see. He was referring to abortion."

"Ab-what?"

"Yeah, women used to eliminate the undesired collection of cells if they were raped by family members, or strangers, or for health reasons."

"For health reasons?"

"Yeah, well, they also terminated their pregnancies if they couldn't handle it emotionally or financially or mentally…or if they were too young, too old, it wasn't the right time, they weren't in the right coupling. Lots of reasons."

"You mean like…voluntarily?"

"Of course."

"And they used cleaning products?"

"Anything they could find, but chances were they could take a pill or a doctor would scrape out the uterine culmination."

"Culmination? You mean a baby?"

"Technically an embryo, then a fetus."

"That's gross."

"Some would call it that, others would say it's freedom of choice. Some would also view what we did at the Commune, assigning rightful owners, as wrong and disgusting. Factory-produced babies in a line-up of human uteruses in vitro would also be gross to a few."

"To be honest with you—"

"Gross," said Rake.

Samara picked up her chicken and with the other hand she held onto Rake's arm. Man, she was becoming fond of this guy.

Chapter 23

THEY TOOK TURNS SWEEPING. It was a mess. Dust everywhere, rat droppings, cat urine. There was a cat? Where was the cat?

She spotted a tangled pile of rope in the corner and jugs and metal wire. Her mind was racing, thinking of practical uses for each thing they found. They could stay here for a while. It wasn't too far from the ocean. Tony could easily make the trip a couple of times a week to pick up his salt water. She herself didn't want to go back. It had been too disturbing.

So far so good; they were three, they had lodging, until the owners came back, if they came back. When and if that happened they would decide what to do. They could build a second house somewhere nearby. Would the well be enough? Maybe they should look for a pond, a stream. The river wasn't close enough. She didn't know anything long term, but for now, this minute, this was good.

Once the place was decent enough Samara decided to go strolling, only through their lot, of course. She was scared to death of what else she might find out there. Everyone they'd met had seemed cracked somehow. She had once thought herself to be damaged, but no more. She was loved. She felt it. Or at the very least, wanted. Wanted was good. Her lack in the upper region didn't matter to him. They were just scars. She'd survived, and she felt better than she had in years.

Twenty yards down the lot there was a mound with two pieces of wood on it. It looked like the thing her mother loved, except bigger. What was it Tony had called it? Cross. Like a wide X, except standing on one of its legs.

Samara sat down in front of it. She wondered what was underneath. Engraved on the wood were the words: Gloria in Excelsis Deo. What language was that? It wasn't English, that much was sure. She stared at the letters and tried to sound them out.

Rake walked up behind her. She had heard him coming, the scraping gait, making the grass and dirt vibrate.

She put her hand on his without looking up and declined her cheek into it.

"Tony good?"

"Is Tony better? Can he stay in the house?"

"Yes."

"There's two bedrooms. What do you think? It would be safer if anyone were to come around."

"Guns."

"You found guns or we need guns?"

"Found. Kitchen."

"Really?! In the kitchen? That's wonderful. I'm a great shot."

"Kill?"

"Have I killed? Yes, many. Innocent people. Children, even. Freedom seekers. Pretenders."

"Why?"

"It was my job. It was the world around me. I didn't know it was wrong. I mean, I felt it inside me when I was by myself, but it was all I knew."

"Bad."

"Yes, I feel sick to my stomach. I felt sick about it even then. I'm a killer, Rake. Are you sure you want to be with a killer? I should have asked you before we got married, but you can leave any time. Our marriage is a fantasy."

"No." He turned to leave.

"Wait."

"Come," he said and headed back to the house.

"Hey, Tony, what's inside the pile of dirt over there? And what do the words In Ex Deo-something mean?"

"In Excelsis Deo! Great song."

"Song? Where can I hear it?"

"We'd need a gramophone or a piano or a player of some sort. And we have no electricity sooo…it's not gonna happen."

"Do you know the words? Could you sing them? Could you write them down?"

"No singing for me, but sure, I know portions of it."

Rake watched Tony closely as he wrote out the lyrics she wanted. He went over to him, took the paper and pencil out of his hand and brought it to her.

"Words," he said, imitating Tony's scribbling.

"You want to learn?"

"Yes."

"You want to write? Of course. And you must learn to read in order to write."

"Yes."

"Okay, we'll do a few lines each day. You seem to be a quick study based on your speaking progress. Tony has two books with him. We can start after dinner?"

"Morning," he said and took Samara's hand.

"Sure…" He was bringing her to the bedroom.

"Eat."

"You want to—?"

"Take."

"You want to take me?"

"Yes."

"You want to ravish me?"

"Now."

Rake turned unapologetic, brutish and gentle all at once. He had her in the bedroom, with Tony a few yards away.

"I'll be out in a second," said Samara, examining the piece of paper with the lyrics on it.

Angels we have heard on high
Sweetly singing over the plains
And the mountains in reply
Echoing their joyous strains

Gloria in excelsis Deo

Come adore on bended knee
Christ the Lord, the newborn King

Repeat refrain Gloria

(That's all I remember)

"Hey, Tony," she said, entering the living room with the sheet in hand. "This is beautiful."

She stopped short. Rake and Tony were polishing a pile of weapons. There were firearms, bows with arrows, hatchets.

"Wow, that's a lot of bang."

"Yeah, the guy who lived here, the people who lived here…seems they liked guns. Or felt they needed them."

"Well, clearly," said Samara, approaching. "There's a lot of psychos out there."

She swayed, lost her balance and grabbed the table, rattling the steel. Rake put his arm around her waist and walked with her to the couch.

"Wrong."

"I don't know what's wrong. Not feeling so good. Help me to the bathroom please. Or to a bucket."

Samara hunched over the pail in the corner. She felt like she was going to throw up, but nothing came. She thought about what Mr. Umbrella or…Niger had said. He'd asked her if she was pregnant. And the kids had called her mama. She wondered, could it be possible after so many years of blockers? Hadn't there been harm done? Permanent harm? She brushed it aside for now, but it was in the back of her mind. She'd be careful. Just in case.

She remained on the couch and elevated her feet. She dared not touch her stomach, though she wanted to. There was a pull to place her hand there. How would she feed it anyway? She had no milk, would never have milk. It couldn't very well eat fish. Holyshh— a part of her wanted it. Wanted to be pregnant. To be a mother.

"Water?" said Rake.

"Yes, please."

He brought her some water, leaned over and kissed her forehead. What a guy. So nice. She hoped it would last. She hoped it was real.

Tony was watching her, silent. "Here," he finally said. "This one's perfect for you. Light enough, and powerful." He handed her a Glock, 9mm. She checked the magazine. Seventeen rounds. It would do.

Rake picked up a Beretta 93R and aimed it out the window. "Good."

She placed her gun on her stomach and raised her legs to the coffee table. "I like it here. Maybe we should scrounge for seeds. Anything that we could grow. Where's my chicken?"

"Out in the yard. There's still feed scattered around under the dirt. It's picking. Seems to know its way around."

"Cool," said Samara and lay her head back.

"You sure you're okay?"

"Yup. Just give me a minute."

Each day they went out for food. They made slingshots and set snare wire, killed birds and ate fish that Tony brought back from his treks to the beach. They improved the house and tilled the garden. No seeds yet, but who knew what they would find.

They scavenged and picked berries. The wild mushrooms they unearthed they tested on their lips before eating. Milk was lodged in the back of her mind.

They got on well enough, the three of them. Tony kept mostly to himself, but watched them respectfully from a distance. He had moved back to the shed, fixed it up and made it his own. He contributed steadily to the food supply and helped Rake with the upkeep of the house and surrounding lot. She cooked what she could and cleaned and tended to the empty garden. Not one among them knew how to make things grow.

Rake was her Rake. Heated and helpful and caring and beastly. Each time she looked at him she was puzzled and moved. Her friend, her partner, who had made her a living, breathing, loved woman.

"Have you seen or heard or smelled any farm animals on your hunting trips, like maybe a cow?" she asked him one day as they were eating lunch. "I've seen nothing at all, but you…I don't know…who knows. I really want milk. Craving it."

"Milk," said Rake, with a pensive look on his face.

"Almond tree! That has milk, doesn't it? Could you help me look for one? There's so many kinds here that I can't tell the difference."

"Yes. Come. Go now."

"Do you mind if I rest a bit more? I might have caught a bug, not sure, but I'm beat. Later? Tomorrow?"

"Rest."

When Rake was gone, Samara leaned her head back and closed her eyes. After a while she smelled something in the air, felt a heat source nearby. She unfolded her eyes. Tony was standing in front of her, his crotch near her face. He was holding a rifle.

"Tony, I didn't hear you come in. Don't stand so close please. Your boils haven't been gone that long and…I just don't want."

She heard the entrance door hit the wall before she saw him. He looked at Tony and at her. His eyes narrowed. He came closer and extended his hand. "Found."

"You found an almond tree!? Wow, that's amazing. I'm feeling better. Let's go!"

They moved around Tony, still careful not to touch him.

"Look," He pointed up to a tree ten yards into the bush. "Close."

"Yes, and it's full! They're not ripe yet, or are they? I wouldn't know. They have green fur. That's why I didn't notice them earlier. Looks just like any other tree. Rake, you're wonderful." She turned around and kissed him over and over. He held her and spoke quietly in her ear. "Kill."

Her heart skipped a beat. "You're not a killer, Rake."

"Yes."

"You are a killer?"

"Yes. Good."

"You're a good killer?"

"Good man."

You're a good man and a killer?"

"Yes. Kill bad."

"You kill bad people?"

"Yes."

"Okay…"

"You mine."

"Okay." Wow, she didn't know Rake. Hardly, and they could barely communicate. But she was learning more every day as his speech improved. She was aroused. "Take."

He bent his face into her neck first, took his tongue out, and licked her like a dog. He moved his way down to her chest where nothing was, and he kissed. Small pecks. On the scars. And over her heart. And he took her. Hard, like a drumbeat, perfectly. She reached a strange kind of height, a flight, a capture and a release. Wow, this man. This man. All man.

"Love," he said as they walked back.

"Love," she said.

He stopped walking and turned to look at her. "Love."

"Yes, love."

Tony was nowhere to be found when they got there. They heard shuffling outside about an hour later. They smelled a fire and something cooking and went to see. He had brought mussels, and shrimp, and crabs.

"Thanks," said Rake, and went to help him. "Good catch."

"Wow," said Samara.

They ate like kings and wolverines. They laughed and joked, and Tony stayed on his side and Rake and Samara on theirs. It was good. They had housing and food and company.

The next day Rake came back from the woods with what looked like a big rat. "What is that?" she said.

"Good food."

They roasted it and ate. Samara thought she saw eyes in the foliage around them. "Did you guys see that?"

"The movement? It's the wind."

"Nah, I think I saw eyes. I think we're being watched."

"Well, we have enough firepower," he said and touched the rifle next to him.

Samara leaned back into the gun tucked in her pant waist. "Maybe we should put up a fence. I think I saw some wire around,"

"Sure, we could do that."

"No," said Rake. "Trapped."

"Hmm…we could be trapped… Maybe we should take turns standing guard at night." She turned on her side and closed her eyes.

When she woke she was in her bed, and it was morning. Someone was brewing what smelled like coffee.

"Hey, is that coffee?" she said, stumbling into the kitchen. Tony had moved back in, it seemed.

"It's chicory. Almost the same."

"Smells good."

Rake was sitting on the couch facing the door, and she sat next to him. He placed his hand on her knee. With his left hand he accepted the offering from Tony.

"This is delicious. Thank you," she said and smiled gratefully when he brought her a cup as well.

"Mama."

"What did you say?"

"Nothing. I just gave you the coffee."

She turned to Rake. "Did you say anything?

"No."

"I swear I heard 'mama.' Just like in the woods, Rake, with that weird man and the kids. The ones without clothes. Remember? The gray ones."

Samara was starting to panic. What was that? Was someone else here? Had they been following them? It was several miles…not super close. Holyfriggs—she wasn't sure about this place any more.

"Calm down. It's nothing."

"Are you out of your mind telling me to calm down? I know what I heard."

Samara grabbed her stomach, and leaned over. "I think I'm going to be sick."

"Have you been bleeding?"

"What a strange question, Tony. I mean, seriously."

She threw up all over her shoes and the floor in front of her. "Sorry. I thought I had it under control. I didn't know it would actually happen. Sorry."

She tried to get up to clean her mess, but she felt lightheaded.

"Wait," said Rake. "Sit." He rose, got the mop and cleaned what he could. He took it outside to rinse and came back in to finish the job.

"So sorry. Thank you, Rake," she said weakly and exhaled.

"Well, have you? I'm a nurse, remember? You're face is bloated, your eyes are glossy, and you look pregnant."

Samara was speechless. Rake had stopped what he was doing. His eyes locked on Tony who made a half-circle motion over his stomach. "Baby. Pregnant."

Rake's pupils, like big dreams, sought Samara.

"My stomach is completely flat. Yes, I've had a trickle, very slight, but don't ask me any more questions. Enough of this nonsense." She turned her face away, but she knew deep inside. She felt different. Like something was there. Someone was there. There was a leap in her heart, which terrified her. What was it? Was she happy? Was she thrilled? Was she full? Why did she want to cry? Was it from joy? What was she going to do? How could she bring a baby into this world? This horrible, unbelievable world where they burn you and brand you and cut your breasts off and follow you and everybody wants something, a piece of you. How could she so badly want it despite everything? Despite all the horror. How could she feel so alive and breathing? Is that why she wanted milk? To find milk? Did she already know in her core, on her skin, in every bone in her body? Was she? Wasn't she? She'd feel relief if she wasn't, and thunder and lightning if she was. An earthquake enough to make the world shake, come apart. She would make it tremble.

She felt power inside her. Was it true? She really wanted to know.

"How can I find out for sure either way?"

"There's a test back at the Commune but nothing I know of here."

"Wait," said Rake.

"Wait?"

"Yes, wait." He went up to her, bent down, and kissed her stomach. He sniffed her. Tony watched.

"Okay, guys, we have to fortify, if we're staying."

Samara touched Rake's hair, and he rose.

"I don't want to stay," she said. "We can find another place without those warped kids and that madman so near."

"Well, let's wait to see if you're pregnant."

"No. Let's go now. We'll find something else. Somewhere better."

"We're go. You come."

"Okay, fine," said Tony. "Let's pack up what we can, make some kind of pulley, and take as much as we're able with us. Fruit, fish. We can smoke it all night and have it ready by tomorrow. I'll stand guard outside."

"Almonds," said Samara. "Lots of Almonds."

"Which way do you want to go?"

"Nowhere near the Commune, please."

"More south," said Rake.

"Sounds like a plan."

Too bad. Samara was enjoying the shelter, the food, a bit of stability. But it was just weird for her, those eyes, the sounds, the feeling of being watched. And how did they know that she was pregnant? Was she pregnant?

The chicory was making her feel sleepy. She forced herself to get up and help with the packing, smoking, and gathering. "We could take two carts."

"Two," said Rake as he cut wood. They had found in a pile next to the shed one wagon without a handle and a wheelbarrow with a broken wheel. Rake was making a new one. "Fix."

Samara watched the smoking fish, making sure nothing caught fire. She took some moss and put it in her pocket, in case she wasn't pregnant and the trickle returned.

She bent over and threw up again. This was getting tiresome. Then she saw them. Two pairs of eyes, clear as day. Blue-gray. In broad daylight.

"Guys, could we like get out of here today, not tomorrow? I just saw two more of them looking at us."

"Kill bad."

"Rake, you don't want to kill children, no matter how bad they are. Believe me, I've done it, and it never leaves you. You wind up on the floor not knowing why you're crying. We don't want that. It destroys you in the end."

Rake glanced at her without saying a word more and kept on working.

She was feeling pretty useless and lightly embarrassed for doing the least amount of work. But she wasn't feeling herself. Maybe it was all in her mind, but maybe it wasn't. What if there was a one in a million chance for her to conceive and it never happened again? After all the messed up stuff they'd done to her, and all the messed up drugs they'd given her, who knew what kind of damage there was in there. She didn't want to risk losing it. How could she want it so much? How?

By evening they were ready. The fish were mostly smoked and the crabs and shrimp charred. They'd made an extra wheelbarrow out of sheet metal from the roof of the shed, and Rake had completed the new wheel for the other. She would pull the wagon, packed lightly with plastic bags and extra clothes they'd made. The rest of the load, the fruit and fish, and the heavy water the two men would transport. They each also had a makeshift knapsack on their back. She had a small one, with her almonds, a bottle of water and a thin blanket.

"Are we ready? Can we go? There's no sun, but the moon is full, and the stars are bright."

"My, you're getting to be a romantic."

"Cut it out, Tony."

"Tony. Friend," said Rake looking at him with no expression on his face. She wondered what he was thinking. He sure could master the poker face.

Chapter 24

THEY HEADED OUT, ALL packed up, in single file, with Samara in the middle. Tony was in front, Rake behind her, a knife in his hand. She had her gun in her back waistband, and Tony held his rifle. They'd hidden the rest of the weapons in a hole under the sink and covered it with a sheet of plastic they found in the closet. She decided to leave the chicken behind. It had survived before they came, and it would be fine after they left. It wasn't really hers, anyway. Besides, she reasoned, she kind of saved its life. If push came to shove, she knew they would have ended up eating her.

It was dark, and the moon occasionally hid under the clouds, which made it even harder to see where they were going. Tony attached a string to his belt, and she held onto it. Rake had his hand on her back, grazing it gently. She could hear him breathing.

"You kay?"

"I'm cold."

"Bit more."

"Okay, I can go a bit more."

They walked on by the light only of the sky.

After what felt like many hours, many miles, Samara sat down in the dirt. "I'm finished. I need to stop."

They made a fire in the middle of nowhere. It was windy and cold. "I felt a drop. The fire's going to go out. The food will get wet."

Rake pulled out some garbage bags they'd packed. He tore the side seams and covered his wheelbarrow and her wagon. He made knots over the rims and put small rocks on them. He took two more bags and made a hole at the top. He put one over his head. Samara did the same.

He gave one to Tony who had been watching him.

"Good idea. Thanks."

"The fire?" She had been useless this whole time. She was just constantly tired. Could it be the chicory?

Tony found a few long branches and formed a circle with the tops touching. He took string he had salvaged from the yard and tied them together at the ends. He signaled for Rake to bring him more bags and spread and placed them around the outside of the arranged sticks.

"My boils are dry. Pretty sure I'm not contagious anymore, and my word I won't touch you."

"Okay," said Rake.

The three of them went inside the small makeshift teepee. There wasn't much room, and Tony sat on his side of the fire, and Rake and Samara on theirs.

"I think the fire is burning them even more. They're barely there."

"Good. I'm glad to hear that."

"Eat. Sleep," said Rake.

He passed around the food which he retrieved from his wheelbarrow outside. It was pouring, and he was soaked when he came in.

"No fire while we sleep," said Samara. "Too risky."

Rake used his knife and opened the hole above them more. "Too cold. Small fire."

They ate in silence surrounded by the drizzling hum, beat from the day's walking. From the moving. The nonstop moving.

The next morning they woke damp and shivering. It had rained hard during the night, and water had entered through the sides and top. A thin film of plastic wasn't going to do it. They would have to find a tarp or make one.

They shook the rain out of the bags over the wheelbarrows and the wagon and put them back on.

The sun was strong and dried them as they walked.

"My head is burning. I need a hat. We all need one," said Samara.

They stopped, found some leaves and flexible branches and got creative. The hats were lopsided, but they did the trick.

"Tarp too, please," she said.

The two men tripled-layered some bags, roped them at the corners and folded the thick sheet over the wagon.

They kept on going.

"Where?" said Rake.

"I don't know, buddy. We move forward until we see somewhere livable."

They walked until it was dusk when they all three made a tent. This time they placed the fire outside, near the opening entrance and sealed the top with tape.

They gorged themselves that evening. "Starving," said Samara. No one had noticed, but her stomach was swollen. Maybe it was nothing, but her pants undoubtedly were tighter at the waist.

They had been on the road for weeks now. Their carriers were getting lighter. "Our food supplies won't last long," said Tony. "We have to find some kind of stream, a pond, a river where we can fish. And we need a map. We have no idea where we are. We might be going in circles."

"No circles. Know."

"You know? Okay, lead the way." He waved his arm in front of him.

They packed up and walked on. "Friend," said Rake and went ahead of Tony.

He stayed close to him as they continued on. Samara was advancing slower and slower. Rake looked back at her, winced, and went and took over her load. He pulled both the wagon and wheelbarrow. She carried her backpack.

There were dirt hills all around now. "I think we're lost." She dropped and lay on her back. "I'm done." She looked up at the sky and into the distance. There was a black line like a pole atop a mound. Was she seeing things? "Over there," she said, raising her limp finger. "It looks out if place. Could be human-made. We should go there." She released her head onto the dirt, too tired to hold it up any longer.

Rake started moving stuff from the wagon and piling it onto his wheelbarrow. He looked at Tony. "Mind?"

"No, go ahead."

Rake deposited the remainder of Samara's things on Tony's. He picked Samara up and sat her gently in the wagon. He took his jacket off and made a pillow for her.

"Thanks," she said, peering with half-open eyes, trying to understand what was inside this kind man of hers.

He turned around to look at the far-off mountains. "Let's go."

He pulled her in the wagon with one hand and the wheelbarrow in the other. Over his shoulders was his pack. His muscles flexed as he moved. Their up and down, in and out, lulled Samara to sleep.

"I can walk now," she said when she woke. You'll burn yourself out. Thank you."

They stopped, and she got out. She took the wagon from him. "Look. It's still there. We're getting closer. Can we go? There might be food and water. Maybe some people. Good people."

Rake and Tony said nothing. Sunburned, dirty and sweaty, they bent their head toward the shade at their feet and pushed forward.

They walked until sundown and stopped again to eat and sleep. They had very little food left. Aside from a few rotted pears and some shrimp, which smelled awful, they only had the almonds.

"We have to eat them," said Tony.

"No," said Samara.

"We're low on water. We're really low on food. You look like a skeleton."

She thought she heard a low rumble from Rake. A soft warning under his breath.

They all three were skinny, and their water was almost gone. But she wanted to keep the almonds. Her almonds. In case…just in case. She was bigger around the waist, but the rest of her was all bones. She had unbuttoned her pants many days back. How long had they been gone from the house? She didn't know. Two months, three months? The heat was getting to her head. She couldn't remember. But she was hungry. All the time.

They ate what they had left, the two men famished like her. Rake was getting taller. He was bigger than her now. How was that possible? When did men stop growing? Men without man-made hormones in their body. He was still shorter than Tony, but strong. His muscles rippled and pulled each time he used them. His shirt was tight, forcing against his arms and chest. His pants were well above the ankle, and he'd had to cut holes in his shoes at the tip.

"Here," she said and gave Rake one almond. "And here." She handed one to Tony.

"Are you for real? We're hungry! Like really hungry!" Tony lunged for her knapsack which she kept by her side at all times these days.

"No," said Rake.

Samara screamed.

Tony took off with the bag. "Catch me if you can," he said as he popped almonds into his mouth.

"You jerk! Give them back. You selfish animal. You've always been selfish. Give them back!" She ran after him, but he kept moving around and stuffing his face.

"Now," said Rake loudly, the knife in his hand.

Samara stopped short. "No, Rake! Let it go. No more. I've done enough killing for the both of us. No more."

Rake growled under his breath. "Go."

Tony looked at him and stopped eating. "What? Here, bruh, the rest's for you." And he threw a handful of almonds in front of him. He turned the bag upside down and shook it. "Look, sorry, I don't know what got into me. I guess hunger will do that to you. And all this seriousness is depressing. Lighten up."

"Go. Take things. Go."

"No, man, take it easy." He glanced at the knife in Rake's hand. "You aren't going to seriously hurt me over a few almonds?"

Rake began walking towards him.

"Hold on, man. I'm the only reason Samara has a uterus. I saved her. They were going to take it. Give me a break, man. I saved her."

Rake stopped walking. "Take things. Go. Gut you."

"You're going to friggin gut me? Are you for effen real? I'm bigger than you," he said, his voice slowing down as he processed Rake's face and his blade.

"Listen man, I don't want any trouble. I mean, sorry for the grief. I'll take my things and go."

Samara had been crying, on her knees, mud all over her. It had started raining again, and she watched as her almonds, what was left of them, sank into the wet dirt.

Tony took his wheelbarrow and walked away, looking back occasionally, his eyes pleading, how could you guys kick me out after all I've done for you?

"Come," said Rake, giving Samara his hand and pulling her up. "It's okay."

They searched through the wet earth for the remaining almonds. They found only twenty. He had eaten the rest. Samara put them in her pocket, and took the handle of her wagon. She and Rake pushed through the downpour.

It got darker and darker. Eventually it stopped raining. An hour later they saw a flash of lightning, and it started again.

"Let's stop, please," she said.

Together they made a tent. Water was seeping in through the sides. She placed cut-open bags on the ground around the edges.

"Fire," said Rake.

"What do we have that that we could spare?"

He pointed to the cloth bag that had held the almonds. "Okay. And we can use a trash bag as fuel." Her face was dirty, and her eyes were red, and her voice was rough from all the screaming she had done earlier.

In the morning they took off, heading towards the long dark line she had seen rising into the heavens.

"It's okay," said Rake.

"Yes," she said.

Chapter 25

As she looked into the vast terrain she saw a dark dot, seemingly out of place. It appeared to be moving.

"Look there, Rake. Do you see it?"

"Yes."

The round shape was getting bigger, and it now looked like a smudge. It grew more as they walked towards it.

It was a man. He had a cane and was limping. He was crunched over, as if he had a hunchback.

"He's coming to us."

"Yes." He grabbed her arm and held her back.

The man approached but didn't stop. "The forcers, the forcers, the forcers, oh my Lord, the forcers."

He kept on walking and passed right alongside them.

"Excuse me," said Samara. "Hello."

"Oh my, oh Lord, watch out for the forcers."

"Do you know where we can get water?"

The man turned around. "Water? Yes, water. Lots of water in town."

"Where town?"

"Over there." He pointed left of the wire on the mountain.

"Thanks," said Rake. "Where you go?"

"Away, very far away." He shuffled off at a quick pace like he was being chased, mumbling again.

"We didn't ask him what the forcers were."

"No chance."

What was happening to Rake? His speech was incredible. I guess he just never had the chance to talk before. She was impressed. She liked it; it would be great to know his thoughts and not be surprised all the time.

They stopped again after many hours and set up a tent. She lay outside and Rake came and sat next to her. He lifted her head onto his lap and placed his hand on her stomach. "Yes?"

"Yes."

"Okay."

They slept together in the open tent, snuggled next to the fire, with what was left of their gear nearby.

"We need more water," said Samara when she woke. They had been drinking water they'd collected during the last rainstorm, but it was almost gone. She exhaled and dug into her pocket. She took out the remaining almonds, rubbed them against her shirt and gave half to Rake. "Eat."

"No. You."

"Please."

He took most of the dirt off and put them in his mouth all at once. She ate hers slowly.

"Love you," he said.

She leaned into him and breathed deeply.

That night Rake held her against the world. She thought she could feel him shake, but it was cold. She didn't ask. Let him be, her protector, her man, her beast.

They rose with the sun and headed in the direction of "the forcer" town the old man had told them about. They needed food and water. Their options were few. They had to find civilization, at least for a while, to get some supplies. They had arrow points to trade with, and the wheelbarrow or the wagon. One was enough.

They lumbered on, tired and hungry, in the merciless sun.

"Where are we? I thought we'd be there by now."

"Shh…" said Rake, putting his finger to his lips. "Listen."

She heard a high pitched voice in the distance. It was male. They marched ahead.

"Stay. Wait."

"No, I'm coming with you."

"Please. Stay."

"Okay."

She leaned on the wagon, empty save for some clothes and kindling they'd found along the way. Her gun she had at her back still, under her shirt. There was no way she was trading that.

Rake returned after a short while. "He say, 'Take your pick.' Man, suit, sign, people."

"Okay, good to know. Any guns? Army? People eating each other? Anything dangerous?"

"I think safe."

"Okay, let's carry on. If you sense any danger or I do, and we lose one another, we can meet up at that peak. See that black line over there, the one we saw earlier?"

"No. You with me."

He put his hand on her back and grabbed her shirt.

"Sheesh, Rake. Okay."

As they went nearer the noises became louder. It sounded like…weeping, and a man's nasal voice booming over it all. "Take your pick, take your pick. Today is your lucky day. You get to take your pick! Choice is a lovely thing! Pick, pick, take your pick. Right on up, take your pick!"

"Holymm…what is this?" she said under her breath, and they kept walking towards food.

Chapter 26

THE TOWN SEEMED LIVELY enough, and clean, with trees and shrubs and flowers. People were walking here and there on errands, perhaps, looking busy. Some were sitting on the edge of a fountain with a stone carving of an eagle in the middle, eating their sandwiches and talking.

The town was on an incline. They had tired coming up the last mile or so, but the distant pin far off to the right did look closer. It was high up on a mountain.

On the left of the fount there was a man standing on a podium with a stick like a magician's wand in his hand. He was chanting "take your pick" to a group enclosed in a square. It was flimsy and consisted of a green and purple rope. Next to the speaker was a sign with red lettering. A list.

1. Juicy Lucy

2. Flap your wings

3. Bing bang bop

The people within the corded enclosure seemed distraught. Some were crying, some looked angry, others subdued.

"What is this?" Samara asked the woman next to her who was watching the spectacle. "Is this a show? A lottery? Why are they crying?"

The woman turned to her and licked her ice-cream. "It's the Fifty-time. My turn is next year. You seem to be far off. If you don't mind…" She moved closer to the speaker.

"Let's go," said Rake. "Need water."

"There's juice on the table."

"Take your pick. Time to commence. Take your pick! Line up ladies and gent, and take your pick."

A woman in her fifties? Forties? walked up to him.

"Which shall you have, dear?"

"I want to flap my wings."

"A fairy bird! Here you go, right this way." He led her to a wide sewage-type hole in the ground. He handed her a small pinwheel, colored like a candy cane. "Here you go, girl. Fly!"

She took the little wheel in her right hand, put her left foot in the hole, and she was gone.

"Rake, what just happened?" Samara's breathing had slowed. "What was that?"

"Go."

"No, wait please."

"Step right up, step right up, take your pick, take your pick!"

A pretty, middle-aged woman with red hair walked up to the speaker, dry-eyed. "Give me the poison."

"Oh, you want Juicy Lucy! But of course." He handed her a cup of pink juice from the table beside him.

"See you in hell," she said and chugged it.

After a few seconds, two attendants came on either side of her and led her away.

A woman with a gray bun was next. She was crying hysterically. "Please, I have grand-children, and I'm hardworking. I have my own garden. I contribute. I swear, I contribute!"

"Dear, dear, nothing to worry about Now take your pick, darling," the speaker said less jubilantly. "Do you want to fly?"

"No."

"Do you want the juice?"

"No."

"Will you have the Bing bang bop?"

"I can't do it. I am a Faithful. I cannot do it."

"A Bing bang bop, it shall be."

He took off his gloves and his overcoat and put them on the chair behind the stand. He reached over and picked up the gun by the juice cups. He took one small step back, pointed the gun at the woman's forehead, swayed it from side to side, slowly, painfully, as if in a dance, paused, and fired. "Bing, bang, bop," he said with finality, putting his gun down.

A large man with black gloves discreetly approached and dragged the body to the sewer without disrupting the proceedings.

"Next. Take your pick, take your pick, what'll it be?"

They all waited in line, their heads down, to take their pick. Most were women, she now realized. Only one decrepit man.

Samara twisted out of Rake's grasp and walked over to the lady with the ice-cream. "What is this? Why did he shoot her?"

"You're obviously not from here. I already told you, it's fifty day, or take your pick day, or let's clean up the uncontributors day."

"Please explain, and may I please have some of your ice-cream? I haven't eaten in days, and I'm expecting." It was the first time she had said it out loud. It was the first time she had even fully acknowledged it to herself. Her pants barely fit anymore, even with the string she'd added as an extension, and she walked differently and smelled everything more. Too many signs.

"Sure," said the lady and handed her the ice-cream. "Good luck with the baby. Now if you don't mind, I don't want to miss the rest. I have only a year left before my time is up, and I just want to know—"

"I'm sorry," said Samara. She made to leave but turned around. "Are these 'the forcers?' Is that what they're called?"

"The town is called Fierce. Some rebellious types call it Force."

"Okay, I see. Thanks again."

Samara heard another shot behind her as she walked back to Rake.

"They're killing people." She dug her teeth into the melting ice-cream and handed it to Rake. "Water, food, and let's get the hell out of here."

They filled their jugs in the fountain, trying to be quick and inconspicuous, and retreated while keeping their eyes out for food.

"Garbage. These people are eating sandwiches. There may be some half-eaten ones in the trash."

They found almost whole sandwiches and burgers and wraps, some with only one bite taken out of them, an apple, pieces of cheese curds, even a small bag of unopened cookies. She felt like she struck gold with a small, almost-full carton of milk. Someone obviously didn't like the liquid treasure. She sniffed and drank the rest.

They filled the wagon and wheelbarrow and took tamed steps, holding hands and pretending to be normal. This normal, that normal, whoever's and whatever's normal. Not that they were in danger, being fresh and young, but they couldn't get out of there soon enough. Samara wondered as they descended from the hillock city what other "choices" they had in the name of usefulness.

"Don't look back," she said to Rake, spearing her eyes forward with the oddest idea that she would become stone if she turned around. Where was she getting this stuff?

Chapter 27

"WHAT ARE WE GOING to do, Rake? There has to be someplace we can go and just be peaceful. Maybe we could return to your house?"

"Peace? No thing. Let's go. House bad. Not mine."

Okayyy…so the house they found him at wasn't his. She knew so little about him, but she'd waited this long, and he seemed uncomfortable. His vibe said no more questions please. You never knew what nightmares each person had lived. She didn't want to dig in theirs, and she didn't want them poking in hers. "Let the dead bury the dead," her mother had told her once. And then she said, "Go."

Rake, you know, I like your words. Did you used to speak? I mean, when you were little, with your parents?"

"I did. Not like you. Deaf speak."

"Okay. And you're remembering?"

"Learning."

They walked for most of the day and camped as the sun was setting. They were decently far from Fierce now and only occasionally heard a distant gunshot.

"Some coming," said Rake and stopped stoking the fire.

He took out his knife. Samara grabbed her gun.

"Forcers, forcers, forcers."

It was the old man they had seen earlier.

"Maybe we should invite him to sit with us. He must be hungry."

"Crazy."

"No, not so sure about that. Maybe just suffering. Lonely. Hungry."

Rake whistled.

"Man!"

Silence.

He hid the blade against the side of the wagon. "Man!" called Rake again.

"No forcers here," Samara shouted. "Come eat."

They heard noises from behind the tent.

"Keep gun."

The man approached and stood before them. He gaped at the food and at the gun in Samara's hand.

"We won't shoot. Have a seat." She patted the ground next to her.

"Here," said Rake and placed a metal fishing box in front of him, away from Samara.

"Who you? Who are you?"

"A man. An old man. Of no consequence."

"You from town sure?"

"Yes. That town."

Rake gave the man some water and a half sandwich. He ate slowly. "Sorry. Few teeth left."

"No offense, but you look way older than fifty. How have you evaded their...party over there? Their juice and their pop-pop and whatever that flying was?"

"Forced suicide. That's what it is. At fifty you have to go. You're a liability, unless you produce. It didn't used to be that way."

"Sooo, that's why you're still alive?"

"Yes, never registered. But they've been cracking down, searching the houses, all the back rooms."

"Terrible," said Rake.

"Where will you go now?"

"I don't know. All I've ever known is there. My grandchildren are there. My wife they just— She said she'd refuse to do it. I heard a gunshot. Maybe they did it to her. I left. I left her. I'm a coward."

"No," said Rake. "Man."

"Do you want to come with us?

"Where are you going?"

"To the dark thing high up on that hill." She pointed into the fading daylight.

"That's a steeple."

"A steeple. What is that exactly?"

"It's the top of a church."

"The top of a church…"

"A church is a place where people worship God."

"I know that word. My mother loved Him."

"Did she?"

"Yes."

"Take us," said Rake.

"I don't know. I don't know you. Are you evil? Creedless? Do you live in sin?"

"Sin?" said Samara.

"Are you married? You look like you're carrying."

She touched her stomach. "Yes, we're married. A friend, an ex-friend, married us."

"That won't do. You need a priest to do it."

"A priest," said Rake.

"Is there one at the steeple?"

"At the church? There used to be. The world has gone to hell and back. Not as many people as there once were. Not sure if there are priests anymore."

"Well, the forcers won't find you if you come with us. We'll be three, and that will throw them off. They'll think you're from where we're from."

"Where is that?"

"Far, far away. And it's much worse than your town. Actually, not sure now that I think about it." She didn't want to give too much information, including the detail that she and Rake were not together long or from the same place. She liked this man, but you couldn't really trust anyone blindly, she knew that fact well.

"Yes," said Rake. "Morning."

He and Samara went in the tent, and the old man stayed outside by the fire. Rake gave him a blanket and an extra sandwich corner and a cup of water. They heard him snoring at night as they held each other. Samara was getting big. She untied the string at her waist. Rake petted her stomach, and like that they fell asleep.

In the morning they ate, drank water and packed up their tent. It was getting colder. The walking seemed endless, the days turning into night, the rain turning into sleet. And the old man followed them. They slowed down from time to time and drank and offered him water. Samara rubbed her back. It hurt. She could no longer pull the wagon. They moved everything onto it and hid the wheelbarrow behind a tree.

They had been moving higher and higher up the mountain without realizing how far up they'd gone. "Wow," said Samara. It's pretty." A single snowflake fell on her.

"It is, it is," said the old man, out of breath and leaning on his cane. "It will start snowing soon. You'd better get up to the church before then. It gets cold up here."

"You think you'll be okay?"

"You make it," said Rake. "Come. You going to make it."

"Yes, my lad, I am."

They walked until sundown and set up camp again. They ate the last of the now-rotting leftovers, and drank some water. It started snowing more, and they made a shelter for the man with branches and bags, and went into their own.

"My back is killing me, Rake. I don't know how much longer I can go. It's starting to feel like an impossible climb."

"Turn."

She lay on her side, and Rake massaged her back, from neck to hip. "Want," he whispered in her ear.

"Hmm…we can't. We have company."

"Sleeping."

He had her patiently, silently, held himself back. She could feel his tension, knew he wanted to ravage her. Good boy, she thought. Good man.

"Almost there?" Rake said the following day to the old man.

"Yes, but I can't go on anymore. I'm done. Too old."

"I will help."

"You help your woman. Leave me be."

"Are you sure?" said Samara.

"I'll inch my way up, or not. I'll just sit here for a spell and look at the view. A perfect place it is."

They left him some water and a blanket and the bags and wood, and bade him good luck.

They climbed on, Rake pulling the wagon, sometimes with Samara in it. After a while she would get up and walk, feeling guilty about all the extra weight he was lugging.

The days passed, and she was getting bigger, and they still hadn't reached the church. She hoped there were people there and they had food and water and were kind. She so wanted her mother's people to be kind.

"What's that?" she said, reaching out for Rake and leaning forward to touch the ground. Holding her hand, he bent over to look. He dipped his fingers in the snowy dirt, brought it to his nose and to his tongue, and spat it out. "Blood."

There was a trail of it going up into the mountain. It got wider and wider the higher they went. Had someone been bludgeoned here? Had there been a sacrifice?

"I don't know, Rake. I'm having second thoughts. All this blood."

"It's old."

"Okay…"

"Have no choice. Need food. Rest. Baby coming. Big."

"How long is it supposed to be in my stomach before it comes out? I don't think I ever saw a real pregnant woman. The babies were produced in the factory."

"Yup, Tony said. In vitro." He turned his head away.

"Yes, in big glass vials with real uteruses inside them, hooked up to machines, you know? At least that's what Oz told me and Tony confirmed. And they had no reason to lie, really."

"No, don't know. Let's go."

"So how much longer? Everything hurts. I'm stretched more than humanly possible."

"Don't know. Sit in wagon. Here." He covered her with a blanket, and he pulled. The church looked closer than the day before, but the climbing was brutal. They had no winter boots or winter jackets. How could they know it would snow? Had they known they might have come up with something… She was feeling delirious and desperate.

They made a fire that night with deadwood they had collected on their way up. It wouldn't last the night, but it was something. They warmed their hands and feet and held onto each other.

"Hungry," said Samara. She was starting to sound like him. Why waste words? He was right. One was enough.

"I know."

He dug into his pocket and pulled out an almond and gave it to her. "Saved."

"You saved one for me? Oh, thank you, Rake." She hugged him and kissed him all over his face.

"Love," he said.

"Love you," she said. And it almost hurt.

She woke to hunger pangs and a turning world. "I'm going to shoot something. There must be some kind of life here. I'll take anything. A wild rabbit. I see birds. Do you think I could get one?" She aimed her gun towards the sky and almost felt back. "Whoa." She sat down on the ground. "Whoa."

Rake made her a simple tent in the wagon. "Go inside. Be back."

He was gone a while. When he came back he was holding a serpent of some kind, with its head cut off.

"A snake." She wasn't sure she could eat it.

"Soup." He peeled the skin off, cleaned out the insides and chopped it up. He emptied the fishing box, filled it with snow and set it on the fire Samara had re-ignited. She ate all her portion, and Rake tried to give her most of his.

"No. It's yours."

They slept soundly that night. She had dreams of blood—blood everywhere on imagined walls around her.

They climbed on. She did not know how many times the sun fell into the horizon. They ate anything Rake could kill and melted snow for water. Samara was growing and held onto his waistband like a religion, the other hand on her stomach. Is this why they had done away with human pregnancies at the Commune? This was hard.

"Oh," she said, tugging at his pants.

"What?"

"It moved. A lot. Like a tumble. Do you think it's okay?"

Rake turned and went on his knees. He fixed his ear up against her stomach and smiled weakly. He looked worn out himself. Bigger and broader but also thinner.

"Healthy," he said and placed a light kiss on her belly.

Samara nodded and held his head against her for a second more.

They pushed on forever and could see the structure above them become bigger. It was probably still a few hours, maybe, but they were almost there.

It was large and imposing and made of concrete, and she thought she could detect hints of color. It had the symbol. A cross. Like the one Rake had made for their wedding. Like the one her mother had buried in the sugar pot. Only this one was huge.

"Tomorrow," said Rake. "We're okay."

Chapter 28

THE FOLLOWING DAY THEY heard a dog barking.

They both got up hastily and packed. "Let's go. I have strength. I heard a dog. There's somebody here for sure. Let's go. I'm excited. People. Maybe they're good. I hope they're good."

Her hands held on for a lifeline as they climbed the rest of the way up, her excitement increasing with every hard-earned step. Finally, she saw a dark green iron gate. There were indeed humans inside. Some were tending a garden, one was sweeping, another wiping down the gate.

"We were expecting you," said a man from under a head covering as they approached. "Greetings."

What relief. This was a much needed welcome. Oh, please invite us in quick, thought Samara.

"What is blood?" said Rake.

"Oh, the blood has you concerned. Rest assured, you are safe. Would you like to come in? I see you're in dire need," said the man looking at her midriff.

"Yes, please, thank you."

He was wearing a brown robe with a loose hood over his head. Was he a…what did the old man call them?

"You p-person God?"

"A person of God, yes, but we are no longer priests and monks. We used to be. But we have been excommunicated."

"Ex—?" said Samara.

"We were thrown out of the church."

They walked down a long, dark hallway. "These are your rooms. Excuse me, will you be sharing a room? Have you received the sacrament? I am not one to judge, but we have made amends and have returned to the faith, whether we are wanted or not."

"Sacrament?"

Rake was silent, his eyes peeled and scrolling left and right, his hand on the knife inside its improvised sheath.

The man in the robe looked at him. "Would you like me to hold that for you? I have a powerful dislike of knives—if you'll forgive me. I shall return it when you leave."

"No."

"Please, I need to rest. Just give it to him."

"I'm Guillaume, but some call me Gill. Have a rest. The left room is for you. Your name?" he said looking at her.

"I'm Samara. This is Rake. Thank you so much for taking us in. We won't stay long. We just need to recharge, and maybe some food and water. We can earn our keep, help around."

He looked at her swollenness then at Rake. "I shall see you in the dining hall at seven. There is fruit and water in the rooms."

The man waited, his hands joined inside the long sleeves of his robe. He looked straight ahead.

Samara touched Rake's hand, and sought his eyes. Please.

Rake pulled out the knife, took it by the blade and gave it to Guillaume.

They waited till he was out of sight and went into one room.

"Not sure."

"I don't know either, but he seems nice enough, and we have no choice, really. Look at me. I'm about to pop. I can't move right now. Let us be agreeable and stay as much as they let us, if they let us. Just enough time to get our bearings. Maybe they have a woman here? I need a woman—to ask her things. Woman things."

Rake studied her stomach. "We ask."

They sat at the small bed. On the nightstand next to it was a huge bowl of fruit with apples and oranges, pears and even a mango. "Where did they get all this stuff? Is it even in season? I didn't see any fruit trees coming up."

"Eat."

They ate two pieces each. Guillaume had mentioned the dining hall. Would they be offered dinner? Samara sure hoped so. She could do with a hot meal.

"This place is big. I wonder if we could go exploring. I mean, after we rest."

"We wait. We ask. We see."

"Okay." She lay her head back and fell asleep instantly.

She woke to bells ringing.

Rake who had been sleeping next to her jumped up and looked outside the window.

"What… what is? Let's go."

"No, please." Samara was groggy from sleep. "We have no watch, and there's no clock in the room. Could be an alert for dinner. Is it seven?"

They washed their face and hands and freshened up everywhere with towels and soap in the modest bathroom in their room. It felt so good. There was even warm water. She splashed her face and combed her fingers through her hair. It had grown to her waist. How long had they been travelling? She didn't know. She had lost track of time, moving from one place to the next, surviving one thing to another.

The dining hall took some looking for, but they followed the quiet chatter and the perfume of…yes, that was cooking. Food. It smelled delicious.

They stood at the entrance of the big room, unsure what to do. "Please, please, welcome, come on in. It is a delight to have young people here. Full of life. Vibrant. Please join us," a chubby man, also in a brown robe, told them with his arms extended and motioning to the chairs on his right.

"I'm Francisco. Very pleased to meet you." He bowed his head and sat down.

"Thank you," said Rake.

"Thank you so much," said Samara.

"Please, bow your heads. 'Our Father, who art in heaven, hallowed be your name, your kingdom come, your will be done, on earth as it is in heaven. Give us this day our daily bread and forgive us our trespasses as we forgive those who trespass against us. Lead us not into temptation and deliver us from evil, for yours is the power, the glory and the kingdom forever. Amen.'"

"Amen," said the men in robes.

"Amen," said Francisco, nodding to the newcomers slowly.

Samara said "Amen" and looked at Rake. She hoped he got it.

"Amen," he said. She had been holding her breath and released it.

"May we?"

"Of course," said Francisco, "dig in."

A parade of forks and knives scraped the plates. It sounded wonderful. The food looked scrumptious.

Roast beef. There was even cheese and potatoes and bread, and vegetables.

Samara ate unashamedly and impatiently. She was curious to know who they were and where they were from, but couldn't stop eating. It had been so long since they'd had a hot meal, much less broccoli!

She glanced at Rake with her mouth full, and he too seemed to be enjoying it. But he ate with his eyes up, watching everyone.

"Are there any women here?" she said, finally, after having filled her belly as much as would fit. She was stuffed and grateful. There was wine on the table, and she took a sip. So full-bodied and rich. Where did they get it? What was this amazing place? It was beyond the beyond of…she didn't want to get ahead of herself. After what they had seen, after all the disgusting, unbelievable, horrid, horrific unhumanity she'd encountered in her life and on their travels, how could she believe all this was good and it was real? But she so wanted to believe. Her eyes moved around the room, to every person there. Not one woman. Where were the women? Oh Lord, where were they? She could really use a woman.

"Women? Oh, no, no women." Francisco seemed sad, and the other men around the room became silent. They truly looked miserable.

"Why no women? Why, sir?" She was beginning to despair and panic. Why no friggin women? She needed a woman. Oh, for eff's sake. What was happening to the women? Where were they? She desperately needed a woman.

"You look upset, Samara," said Francisco. "You have no idea how unhappy we are. All of us. Every single one."

"Why? Why are you upset?"

"It's a long and terrible story, my dear. I'm not sure you want to hear it. Especially in your condition."

"Tell us," said Rake, his voice deep and deadly serious.

"This place used to be a church and a monastery, and later, a retribution consortium."

"A what? Please, just simple words. We've not been around church much, or at all, in fact. Why the gloomy faces? Why no women?"

"We haven't always been here, Samara. We come from different churches and monasteries. We have all been shamed, extracted. That means we are no longer clergy or part of the brotherhood. But we used to be."

"What happened?" said Rake, narrowing his eyes and leaning in.

"We call ourselves the Lovelorns. We all fell in love and were kicked out of our place of worship. Word got around after a botched castration, where the priest died, and the rest left. Took off. Abandoned their posts. We found our way here. More and more came each year. But now it has stopped. We haven't had a visitor in a long time."

Samara didn't know whether to ask the next question. She had to remind herself to keep breathing. What the hell. What did she just hear?

"What castra—?"

"We are eunuchs. We have all been castrated at one time or another. For falling in love. The women, gone. Some of us fell in love with nuns. Others with regular churchgoers. They are gone. All gone. They left when they heard what had been done to us. Who can blame them?" He stopped talking and picked up his glass of wine. The men around the table watched Rake and Samara.

"What is eunuch?" said Rake, breaking the silence.

"They cut off their testicles," said Samara under her breath, barely moving her lips.

Rake's eyes widened, and he moved his hand to his crotch. Horror filled his face. His eyes jumped to Francisco and across the room to the other men at the table. He pushed his chair to get up.

Samara put her hand gently on his arm to stop him.

"Is that the blood we found on the way up?"

"Yes, it likely is. Perhaps. We don't know. There are splatters everywhere, even in the garden. It was like that when Ignatius came. He was the first one. He looked at the man at the far end of the table. "After him we trickled in like the dripping blood of Christ."

Samara cleared her throat, wanting to say something, anything. But what was there to say? She herself was guilty of atrocities.

"We have a good life here. Don't feel sorry for us." He turned to Rake. "We won't do it to you. Don't worry. We would never put another man through what was done to us."

"I'm sorry," Samara blurted. "I'm sorry that happened to you."

Rake darted his eyes around. He looked sick to his stomach, a scowl on his face.

"Very well," said Francisco. "We are here to be of service. We do not have a midwife, but these brothers will do what they can."

"Please get me a woman to help. Please. I don't think I can do this alone. I have no milk. I have no milk!"

"Dear, settle down. What do you mean?" Guillaume from across the table interjected.

She looked at him, desperate. "I have no breasts! They took them! I have no milk for the baby!" She was yelling at this point and rising from her chair.

Some of the men's mouths dropped. They appeared aghast, and commiserating. Others pursed their lips with a straight face, an almost-anger in their eyes.

"We have a goat," said Guillaume. "Sit down, Samara. We will help. We are no longer priests and monastics, but we are men of God. Do you know God Samara?"

"God," she said. She was now sitting, emotionally drained and a bit embarrassed about her outburst. "My mother loved God. I don't know who He is, but she loved Him. She said, 'Oh Lord, Oh Lord,' all the time. I say it too. Like her."

"Well," said Guillaume, "God is everywhere. God is here. God is goodness. God is help. He is inside us. We will help you. He is inside you. He is in that baby in you."

"Okay," Samara said. "Can we go now? May we be excused?"

"Please feel free to roam around."

There was a goat! They had a goat! They had a goat with milk! Oh Lord, they had a goat. Thank God, she thought and bowed her head. Thank God. She did not know who she was thanking, what, where, how, but the desire deep inside her to thank, to thank for something so needed. For life. To preserve life. To let it exist. To give it a chance. "Thank you, God," she exhaled as they walked back to the room. Rake kept his hand on her back.

Later, when they were in bed together he leaned over her stomach and kissed it. "Thank you."

"My gun," she said.

"Where is? Not on back."

"My pants are not attached, so it would fall. I hid it. Under us."

Rake raised his eyebrow.

"In mattress?"

"Under it."

"Okay."

Chapter 29

THE WEEKS PASSED TORTUROUSLY for Samara. She had trouble walking and sleeping. Rake would try to caress her belly and kiss it, but she felt like she was burning up. Her cheeks were stinging. Her whole body felt like it belonged to someone else and also fully hers.

She did her light chores gladly. She could not sit around and watch her stomach all day. It moved when she put her hand on it. She saw a foot. A foot. Oh Lord, what was she going to do?

She moved from room to room slowly, dusting the furniture, the window sills, the paintings of people wearing gilded robes.

The church at the back they said was out of commission and not to bother cleaning it, but each day she inched her way closer. She could not resist.

She stood and pondered the brown door with engravings of children. It looked like they had wings.

It squeaked when she opened it. She hadn't ever been in a church, and she wanted to see it. She thought of her mother, her tormented eyes when they took her away.

Inside, the church was proof of a fallen world. There was dust and blood everywhere, toppled golden chalices on the table, pictures of men with a circle around their head. They had a somber expression on their faces. There was a statue on the floor of a man wearing only a cloth on his lower region. He had drops of blood on his side, covered in dust. On his hands and feet were holes. On his head was an unusual crown. It looked like it was made of nails…or thorns. He was wearing thorns? Oh my goodness, what was this? She walked around behind the figure. More pictures, some huge ones, candles strewn all over the floor, sand scattered. And blood in the sand. Blood on the walls. Was this where the botched job that Francisco told them about happened? Holy… Her heart was beating fast. She was hurting. Her hip felt like it was pulling. Her stomach ached. A sharp pain. It lasted a minute and stopped. She held onto the long, dusty wooden benches, one in each row, and walked forward to the man, fallen over onto his side on the floor. So dirty. She took the rag in her hand and wiped his brow. "There," she said softly. She continued to wipe his face, and his crown, the thorns, each one. She shook out her rag, turned it around and wiped his ribs and his back and moved to his feet. She fell over, onto him, and started crying, her tears dropping over his feet with the holes in them. Another sharp pain. "Oh." She held onto the marble. It rattled. It moved. She didn't want to break it. She'd have to— "Oh." She should go find Rake. Something was wrong. Her back felt like it was being pounded. Her stomach…something was wrong. Really wrong. The pain passed. Her hair had fallen onto the form and made streaks in the dust. She kept cleaning, wiping him, becoming more frantic. Go faster, go faster, clean him, clean him. Oh, another sharp pain in her back. She sat and leaned on him, the statue with the thorns, with the holes in his hands and feet. And another hole on his side. She leaned back on the blood on his rib and slid down and placed her head on it.

She looked up at the ceiling. What beautiful art. Who had done that? It was high, higher than the rest of the building. There were no blood splatters on it. Oh! The pain! Was it happening? Was this it? The thing? Was the baby coming? She had to go find Rake. She turned and held onto the stone to push herself up. Oh! This blow lasted longer. "Help," she called. "Help," she said more loudly.

She tried again to rise, and she succeeded. Oh! A sharp pain. It went on and on. She crouched over the figure and fell on her knees. Another pain came and went, and she bent her face into the statue's. "Who are you? Who are you?" She was crying. This was way more than she could handle. "I'm scared!" she yelled. "I'm scared! Help me!"

The door opened and Rake ran to her. "Find you!" He looked worried. He put his arm under her arm and helped her up. "Walk, girl. Walk. Dangerous pick up. Walk, good girl."

He led her into the hall. "Come!" he shouted. "Come! Now! Baby!"

A cluster of humans ran into the hallway. The fathers, the brothers, running to help.

They took her to her room. Two men in brown were putting clean sheets on the bed. One more came in with hot water. Another put a knife in it.

"I'm going to wash you, Samara, and take off your pants. Is that okay?" said Ignatius. "Do not be concerned. I have assisted many of our animals during their travail."

"Dress. Robe. Leave me a minute."

"Immediately," he said and exited the room.

A man she had not noticed before brought in a large brown robe, same as he was wearing, bowed and left them alone. Rake helped her out of her old clothes and pulled the garment over her head.

"Stay."

"Yes."

"Oh!" she grabbed her side and expelled her breath. "Oh! Call them. Help me! Oh."

Ignatius came in without needing to be summoned. There were four others with him. They had clearly been waiting outside the door. "Alright, Samara, I'm here. Do you mind if the other brothers watch? They would like to learn."

"No!" she yelled, and shrieked right after. When the pain paused she was perspiring and out of breath. "Sorry, please no."

Ignatius turned to the men behind him and waited till they were gone.

"Rake, I will need you to assist. Let us wash our hands. Scrub real hard and pour, here, the alcohol, even under the fingernails."

Rake kept looking from Ignatius to Samara, and flicking his eyes to the door and window.

"It's okay, Rake," she reached for his hand and screamed. It lasted for several minutes. The spasms, the punches, as she thought of them, were getting closer.

"It's my back. I feel it in my back."

"As I said earlier I have only delivered animals. I am deeply sorry, Samara. Perhaps, some music would help?"

"No. Wait, where would you find music? Aaaagh!"

"Oh, the love of my life, she—"

"The love of your life?" She screamed again. The pains were getting closer.

"Rake, I don't think I can do this. I don't think I can do this. I think I'm going to die." She whimpered and gritted her teeth and moaned, and held onto Rake's hand.

He stroked her forehead and got some water in a towel and wiped her face.

"Do you know how far along you are, Samara?"

"No!" She screamed and moaned. She thought she was splitting in two.

"Let me have a look," he said, parting the robe.

Rake grunted, a low growling deep in his throat. Samara turned to face him. "Rake, please."

"I see the head, Samara. Next contraction you need to push."

"Push? What the hell! Aaaaaaargh!" She pushed and with the next contraction which came even sooner she pushed again, harder. She felt herself break in half.

"It's here. Rake, grab the towel, come here, put your hand under, ready, I'm going to slip my hand inside, wipe my brow." Samara screamed and pushed another time. She felt something come out. Relief. The baby? Silence.

Ignatius was holding a pasty and wet, tiny human with a cord of flesh attached to its belly. He turned it face-down. "Rub its back with your two fingers," he said to Rake who looked traumatized by this point. But he did as he was told. Ignatius turned the baby around again and put his mouth over its nostrils and sucked. He did the same on the baby's mouth. Rake caressed the newborn's back with two fingers. Finally, there was a cry, a small cry.

"Good Lord Almighty, blessed be your name. Good Lord almighty. Glory to your name. Good Lord almighty, glory be to your name. Good Lord almighty." Ignatius looked like he was going to faint. "Wet towel, warm. Place the baby here, clean her," he said to Rake.

Ignatius turned to Samara. "You did well, mama."

Chapter 30

SAMARA WAS EXHAUSTED. SHE was overwhelmed. She thought she would fly. She thought she could fly. "Give please," she said.

"Mother," said Rake, bringing the baby over to her after he was done cleaning it. "Baby," he said. "Our. Baby girl."

"Yes," said Samara, reaching for her daughter like she had done it all her life

"I need to massage your uterus," said Ignatius. "To help the afterbirth out."

"What? Do what you want," she said, although she hadn't really understood. Rake watched him for a few seconds, then rested his eyes on the baby and Samara.

"She's opening her mouth. Does she want food?" Samara was panicking, hurting. She was aching from joy. She wanted to cry, but she was so happy. A baby. Her baby. She was a mama. Like her mother.

"I'll ask one of the brothers to prepare some milk," said Ignatius. We'll figure out what to do about a nipple. Quick."

"Ignatius—"

"Yes?"

"Thank you."

He bowed his head and proceeded to leave. Rake walked up to him, put his hand on his shoulder. The monk stopped and faced him. He held out his hand and shook Ignatius'. The two men nodded at each other.

"He crying. Sad."

"Sad he won't be a father? Yes, that's sad. It's a devastating world. Beyond that, but whatever. I'm happy I'm alive. I'm happy I have you, and above every feeling in the world, to have this baby. I don't want to part with her, Rake, ever, but I need to sleep, to rest, to recover. Can you find some kind of basket and put towels in it and around the rim?"

Rake kissed her forehead. "Love," he said and kissed the air over the baby.

"You can kiss the baby, Rake."

"No. Lips not clean for baby."

"You're right. She's fragile."

Samara turned to her side, holding the child and watching the snow fall. After a while it stopped, and the sky looked crisp. She wondered if the winters were heavy here. Perhaps they could stay. The people were kind, they had food, and animals, and milk.

The door opened. "Hello, I'm John. Congratulations. We made a nipple out of swine intestine and olive oil, sterilized it, molded and folded and reshaped it. We had a water bottle from days old. It's plastic. Would you like to try to feed the baby to see if it works?"

Rake took the bottle and examined it and passed it to Samara.

"Thank you, John." She sniffed the thick lining. It smelled like pig. Maybe it was her imagination. Didn't he say they cleaned it? She put the nipple on the baby's mouth and jiggled it. It took a few tries, but she finally accepted it. Samara sighed in relief.

"Glory to God," said John and turned to leave.

Samara watched the baby in awe as she ate. She noticed when she looked up that the leaves in nearby trees were agitated. Was it windy again? She thought she saw a rushing blur. "Rake, can you have a look?"

"What?"

"Outside. I think I saw something moving, not the brothers, not an animal. It looked like a shadow. Different."

"I go. I'll go see."

"Did you get your knife back?"

"No. Find something."

She was deliriously tired. She had just given birth. Given birth…given birth… She never imagined in her life that this would happen to her. Life was full. "Thank you," she whispered.

Rake came back with a piece of sharp metal. "Will fix later. Until, good enough." He slipped it into the empty sheath.

She knew he could communicate well now. She'd heard him. Could it be he just didn't care, that words were not so important to him? As far as she was concerned he could speak in grunts. He was a good man.

She yawned. "We need a baby bed, a wooden thing… a creeb!"

"Creeb?"

"Yes. I don't want to crush the baby in my sleep. Or knock her down."

"Hold?"

"You would like to hold her? Of course."

"You sleep."

Samara watched him as he took the baby in his arms and sat in the chair, wonder in his eyes. He held the bottle and offered it to the child from time to time. Samara felt peaceful, a tenderness inside her she hadn't experienced before. She felt no anger, no regret. Not right now. Perhaps later she would again.

Chapter 31

She woke to a knock.

Rake opened the door with one hand and held the baby with the other. Wow, he was a natural.

It was a swarm of brothers.

"Sorry to disturb you," said Francisco.

"We waited till you had a bit of a rest," added Guillaume.

"How are you feeling?" said Ignatius. "We've brought you some soup."

"May we come in?" John asked with his palms together. The others stood behind them, sneaking a peak into the room.

"Yes. Please." Samara raised herself to a sitting position as painlessly as possible.

Ignatius placed the soup on the table, and they all moved closer to Rake and gazed at the baby in awe.

"You did a great job, Samara," said Guillaume. "You too, Rake," he added, and winked at him.

"A splendid miracle," said Francisco.

"May I hold her?" said Ignatius. Rake looked at Samara. She nodded, and he passed the baby to him.

"My, how beautiful. What beautiful blue eyes!"

They gazed at the baby as if they had never seen one before, like it was otherworldly.

"Truly a gift from God," said Francisco. "Proof that God has forgiven us our sins. See what he brought into our life?"

"Guillaume, you had said something about a sacrament when we came. Do you mean like marriage?"

"Yes, indeed I do. Marriage is one sacrament, baptism another."

"I would like that. To be married in this place by one of you." She looked at Rake.

He nodded. "Yes."

"Maybe with some music, and that statue in there, the room…the church."

"Oh, the representation of the Man-God. He is a God. He is God. In the flesh."

"In the flesh…" she repeated, trying to grasp the concept.

"Indeed, in the flesh."

"We marry again," said Rake, going up to Samara and showing them her finger with the wooden ring.

"Oh, I see. You're already married but would like a religious ceremony. Oh my, that shouldn't be too hard. We have been excommunicated and exiled, but most of us know the ritual, the sermons, by memory, of course. The book was expunged ages ago, but we were gifted with the words when we took our oaths."

"It will be arranged," said Ignatius, giving the baby back to Rake.

"We are asking a lot, I know, and we really appreciate everything, and thank you for the soup, and your kindness—"

"Make a creeb?" said Rake.

"Make a crib?! But of course we can!" blurted a brother whose name she couldn't remember. "Jesus was a carpenter. We are all handy with wood, in Jesus' name, and glory to God!"

"Let us go, gentlemen! We have work to do," said Francisco.

"Me too. I help."

"Thank you," said Samara as they all, including her husband-to-be-again, scuttled out the door.

She heard clanging and banging and sawing and thought she saw a silhouette in the window. She had been through a lot this past year, and the pregnancy, and giving birth. But Samara had seen darkness, had caused enough herself that she knew evil was out there. Everywhere. Maybe even here. How she hoped it wasn't here. She needed to believe. In lightness. She'd just had a baby, and she really wanted it to be a good world for her. Maybe there was hope, wasn't there?

She put the baby on the bed with a pillow on either side and eased herself off as slowly and carefully as she could. Her legs were wobbly. She wasn't sure she could make it, but she had to check. She made her way to the window and faced the world outside. Nothing there. Nothing out of the ordinary. She could see the mountain decline. The snow had melted. What season was it? She hardly knew. They'd barely had a chance to catch their breath. It was one hell of a year. Hell, indeed. But also beautiful. She was not alone anymore. They were three. A family. She looked up. She hoped God was real. She hoped He was looking after her and the baby. And Rake. She thought about the statue in that big room…the rotting church, a broken and bloody house of God. She wondered what horrors had taken place for there to be so much blood. But the ceiling was untouched. She'd have to keep looking up, where all the beauty was.

She walked to the bed where her newborn slept. She took a blanket, placed it on the floor in the middle of the room and gently lay the baby on it. She went back to the bed, kneeled, and squeezed her hand between the mattresses. She felt it. It was there. Her gun. She exhaled and spoke softly to the child. "I will kill anyone who tries to hurt you."

She crawled over and picked her up. "My baby. My beautiful baby." She lowered her head, closed her eyes and inhaled.

There was a knock on the door.

"Come in."

It was Ignatius.

"Oh my, would you like a hand? You shouldn't be getting up. You've been through quite the ordeal. But your body is young. You'll be up and running in no time."

He extended his arms, and she handed him the baby. "The crib is almost ready." He moved the child to one arm and helped Samara up and to the bed.

"Can you hold her for a while, Ignatius? My legs and arms are trembling. I shouldn't have gotten up, but I wanted to look out the window. Have there ever been unwanted visitors? Intruders? I mean, since you came here, after the botched thing with the other priest."

"Not that I can recall, and I would remember if that had happened. We are not the violent type, and we bother no one. We have very little, just enough to survive on, and we are way, way up. It's unlikely anyone will come here to molest us. We were surprised when you appeared, and are thrilled. We watched you climbing, and that man of yours helping you, carrying you, pulling you. Very emotional, indeed, to see the two of you and remember love. And we noticed that you were large around the middle area and assumed…well, we didn't know, but we hoped. Oh how we hoped."

"Thank you, Ignatius." She lay her head back into the pillow and closed her moist eyes.

"Oh my darling, oh my darling, oh my darling, Clementine…"

Her eyes split open, and she glared at Ignatius. She had stopped breathing and had to remind herself. Breathe in, breathe out, go slowly, go smart.

"Ignatius, that's a pretty song. I believe I've heard it before. Where did you learn it?"

"Oh my, it is truly a special song. One may try, but one will never forget. Love. Her beautiful face, her intoxicating sound. She used to sing it, you know. So beautifully, like doves flying into the air, fluttering, coming back down. I believe she made the world turn with her voice. I would have done anything for her. But…I get ahead of myself, and my mind wanders. Talking to the brothers here…well, they have their own pain. Their own sorrows. They don't need to hear mine."

"I like hearing you, Ignatius. You helped me bring my baby into the world. You can talk all you want, anytime you want. I like your words. Please say them. Say. Tell me about the woman."

"Oh, my Clementine?"

Samara's heart skipped a beat. She knew that name. She knew that song. They'd ruined it. Those weirdos with the darling and the branding and the sickening decadence. She was getting angry and clenching her teeth. What they'd done to her…to her back. How freakish. Those freaks. True freaks.

"Oh, Samara. You look angry. Have I made you angry?"

"Oh, no, no, sorry. I just felt pain in my uterus and you know, there," she said pointing to her private area. "I think I may need stitches."

"No no, I checked. A tiny tear. It will heal on its own. As for the womb, it's contracting, going back to its original form and size. You will feel pain for a while, but do not fret. It is normal."

"How do you know so much about pregnancy, Ignatius? Animals can't tell you if they have pain in their uterus. I don't mean to pry, but I am interested, and you are lovely to talk to. I've only been speaking with Rake for the better part of a year, and I adore him, and it's been wonderful, but it's refreshing to hear something new. Completely refreshing." Samara held her breath. *Please tell me, please tell me, please tell me.*

"Oh, it's somewhat embarrassing, but then again, worth every atonement. And I have paid the price. The ultimate price, as you well know."

"You have, and I'm sorry about that. I'm sorry about all you had to go through." *Please talk please talk please talk.*

"My Clementine, she was married and expecting when we fell in love. Fell in love. Sounds like a melody of the finest notes."

"Do you think I could have her now? I feel better."

He handed the child to Samara and put his hand on her head. "Kyrie Eleison," he said.

Oh God, I hope that is good. I hope he said something good. I hope it's a blessing. I hope he's good. I hope he's a good person. I hope that's not some kind of spell, some kind of voodoo or witchcraft or curse. Oh Oh. She was breathing heavily, rapidly.

"Samara, are you okay?"

"Yes, yes, it's just the pain. It comes and goes. Please go ahead."

"My Clementine was married and pregnant with her husband's child when we met. I was serving the Lord in a nearby village, and she would come to pick flowers and listen to the service outside the church. Eventually I convinced her to enter. She began to come for confession and after a while…she didn't want to go home. She said her husband had been with most of the women in town, had fathered many children. He would not be interested in being a father to hers. It would cause problems for the future world, he had told her. She was to have no child of her own."

"Oh," said Samara.

"Are you feeling the pain again? I could get you some tea. It might help. Do you want more soup?" He leaned over to look at the bowl. "Good, good. That is excellent."

"I'm okay. Thank you so much. Your story…"

"Yes, yes, my shame, my story, my light, my hope… Oh, I shouldn't say that. It is a sin. Forgive me."

"Please."

"I hid my Clementine in my lodgings for months. I watched her grow. She read books and explained things about the female body to me. The rest I discovered for myself. With her. With her…"

"That sounds beautiful, that you loved her and helped her."

She knew that town! She knew that bloody guy, that psycho with a million kids! Facticity! That was the name!

She looked up at Ignatius and smiled. "Feeling better now."

"I'm so glad to hear that. Shall I get you some tea, anyway?"

"No, no, I'm fine. Clementine…what happened to her?"

"Well, when they found out that I was communing with…loving…fornicating with…they bludgeoned me. But only after I helped her escape."

"May I ask where she escaped to?"

"Oh, yes, yes. We walked for miles and miles and miles. No one wanted a pregnant woman except this one village that spat on us as we approached. They really only spat at her, my Clementine." He stopped talking again.

"That's terrible. I'm glad you didn't stay." Samara knew that place as well. Those monsters with sick words and vile signs, and the gawking! She remembered. Thank goodness for Toodeloo…

Imogene, who helped her escape. She still felt badly about taking Rake, but not really, kind of…very little.

"It smelled horrible, and they were hateful," Ignatius continued.

"It sounds like it."

"We finally found ourselves at a cliff above a pond, with a waterfall. She was big at this point. There was no way she could climb it. But I searched like a crazy man, and I found a secret path. I helped her almost to the top, and we looked around. Everything seemed peaceful. Civilized. I lifted her up the final step."

"Do you by any chance know the name of that town?"

"I do not. There were soldiers, people in uniform. That much I recall."

"And that was that?"

"Yes. That was that. I do not know if she lives or died. I do not know if the baby survived, whether it was a boy or a girl. I know nothing."

Samara couldn't take anymore. She knew! She knew who that baby was! She knew!!! And that woman who sang her that melody growing up! That woman with the beautiful voice. That woman! Her mother!

Samara burst out crying. "I'm sorry. I'm sorry. I'm so sorry. It's just a sad story. I'm sorry you lost the love of your life. I'm sorry they chopped you up. I'm so sorry."

"Oh, Samara. I am sorry too. But what can one do? What is done is done. And I forgive them. For I too wish to be forgiven for my sins."

"What bloody sins?! That you fell in love?!"

The baby started to cry. Oh no, she had startled the baby. She had upset the baby. Her baby!

"Samara, you are becoming too anxious. I will go, and we shall speak again another time, hopefully about a more pleasant subject as this is clearly upsetting. Someone shall be back with the crib so you can get some rest. See you at dinnertime." And he left.

Not only did they come back with a crib, but with a basket for the child and a box thing with wheels to push her around in.

Rake came in full of smiles. He kissed her and picked the baby up and kissed the air around her.

"Love," he said.

"Love," she said.

"Dinner soon. You like crib?"

"Yes, I love it. Thank you." She had learned a lot. Was Ignatius' lover her mother? It sure sounded like it. And the psycho who ordered her branding her own father? What a horrid idea, but possible. The only thing was she'd never heard her mother called Clementine, or anything come to think of it. But who would keep their name if they were trying not to be found? And she didn't know there was a secret path going up to the Commune!

"Come lie down with me."

Rake took the baby and placed her in the freshly made crib, fitted with half a mattress. He walked over to Samara and lay next to her. He dug his face into her neck.

"Can we?"

She shook her head gently.

"Want. Too soon?"

"Yes," she said and put her hands in his hair. "Too, too soon."

They lay like that for a while, the baby sleeping, and she, stroking her man's hair. This beautiful man. This good man. This hungry man. She felt a need.

For him. She would heal, and they would have each other. For today, this was enough. Guillaume had told her about magic dust inside. A soul, he said. That's where Rake was now, in her special dust, and in her arms.

She thought about all that Ignatius had said. What a sad story. What a story of self sacrifice. And yet she was here. He had helped her be here. If what she had understood to be true— Of course it was. No such thing as coincidence.

The bell rang for dinnertime, and they made their way to the dining hall. All the men were seated around the table. She had never seen them so jovial.

"Let us say a prayer, my brothers and sisters," said Francisco. Everyone joined hands. The prayer was almost jubilant. She loved the words. They were…full. Like truth. She wanted to learn them. She'd ask, and she'd also ask if they knew the Gloria song. She would love to hear it.

Rake dug into his dinner and laughed and smiled at the commentaries. It looked like he was making friends. Good for him. They were praising him for his carpentry skills.

"Like Jesus," he said, turning to her. "Good carpenter like Jesus."

"That's quite the compliment."

"Yes."

The food was delicious and the wine, oh so good.

Guillaume took a fork, clinked it against his glass. "Hosanna! Hosanna to the Highest! We are to have a wedding soon, friends. We must clean the church, restore it, make it shine, glorify the Lord. Glory to God for the baby! Glory to God for Samara and Rake! Glory to God, indeed!"

She smiled. Wow. How good to be wanted.

Chapter 32

SHE COULD HEAR CLAMORING and banging and breaking, and laughter. She settled the baby in her wheelbox and headed to the church. Rake was there, helping.

They had done a tremendous job. The marble monument was gleaming with oil they must have put on it. The blood on the walls was barely visible. In the cleaning they'd taken off some of the paint underneath. The clean windows with different colors of glass were beautiful. The sun came in through them and made the room glow. Wow, what a bunch of men with purpose could do! They were handing each other pieces of wood, oil, soap, a mop. Francisco was dragging a golden round bowl on a stand with wheels. Samara picked up the baby and walked towards him.

"Careful, my dear. There's wood and nails on the floor still. We're not done yet but almost there!"

"Francisco, may I ask what that is? The thing you're holding."

"This is the baptismal pool. For the baby."

"Excuse me? I don't understand."

"It's for the baby's baptism. Have you decided what she will be called?"

"The baptism?"

"Yes, Samara, the christening. All babies must be christened. In Jesus' name. I hope you approve." He smiled and bowed, and resumed pulling.

The baptism…the christening…in Jesus' name. Holy…this was really new. Really something. What was she going to do? What were they going to do? Was it dangerous? She looked around the church and took a seat near the statue at the very front. It was huge. How had they even lifted it? It had cracks and the horrifying holes no longer had real blood on them. Just paint, which was better, she guessed. How would she let her baby look at this as she grew up? Wouldn't she be traumatized? Samara thought of her own childhood and all the things she'd seen around her, what seemed now like horrors. I guess she'd be okay. These men had done so much for her… She stared at the figure for a while longer and waited for something. Was it alive? Was there anything in there? *In Jesus' name…* "Okay, baby girl, you're going to be baptized," she said.

She turned her head to the window. A dark blur again. She counted the men. Were they all here? They couldn't be. Besides the shadow was shorter, much shorter, but upright. She bore her eyes into Rake who was busy working with the brothers.

He stopped what he was doing and strode closer. "What wrong? You look scare."

"I swear, I think I saw something. I'm getting a feeling that something, someone is watching us, Rake."

"Hm." He walked to the window and returned. "Carry gun. Put in baby box under baby. I have knife. Make more."

"Okay," she said, but the killer in her was boiling. Motherhood had made her kinder, gentler, more loving, and too soft. But the old knowledge…the old instincts were starting to resurface. If need be she knew where to find them.

Chapter 33

THE WEDDING WAS VERY different from their first. John made her a white dress from bedding, and curtains for the frills, and she and Rake had real rings fashioned out of scrap metal, heated and pounded to smoothness. On the inside was engraved an S and R and the number seven. It meant protection, Francisco explained. She was okay with that. They were sized to fit perfectly on the third finger of the right hand. She felt special. She had to admit these rituals marked you. They marked your mind. Rake wore a brown suit Timotheus had made him. He looked sharp and seemed to be enjoying it. He was beaming and kept touching the lapel and looking at her and the baby.

The brothers sang hymns and, at her request, In Excelsis Deo. She now knew the words by heart. She had gotten the complete version from Ignatius.

Samara held the baby in her arms and Rake kissed her and the air over the baby when they said the I do's. She couldn't help but be distracted at times, glancing always at the windows.

"Come, my dear, since we are here shall we double the festivities and baptize the baby?" said Francisco.

Samara was somewhat startled. This was quick. "Uhh…" She looked at Rake. "Is this okay with you? Do you agree with it? Should we baptize her?"

"Yes, Samara. Jesus good."

Holy…what had they done to him?

"You're not going to become a monk, are you?" she said, smiling.

"No, Samara. I am yours."

"Okay, let's do it."

When they immersed the baby in the water and she screamed Samara almost went and grabbed her from Francisco. She held back her urge to hit him over the head and run with her child. Rake likely sensed this because he held her firmly by his side.

"A name please. Her name," said Francisco.

Samara looked wide-eyed at Rake. They had forgotten about a name!

"What was your mother's name?"

"Ma."

"I don't know my mother's either." It was mostly true.

"Name, please. Sorry, Rake and Samara. I should have given you time to prepare, but I need a name."

"How about Gloria?" She turned to her now blessed and confirmed husband. "It's a beautiful song and…do you like it?"

"Yes. Perfect."

Francisco nodded his approval. "Alright then. In the name of the Father, the Son, and the Holy Spirit, we baptize you Gloria. May you follow the path of Christ and be protected by Him forever, unto the ages of ages. Amen."

"Amen," everyone said together.

They moved to the dining hall, feasted and drank, and the brothers took turns making toasts to the happy couple, to God, to Jesus, to love. They even toasted to loves lost. Were they getting drunk? There sure was a lot of wine going around.

Later in the room they stood over their baby.

"You beautiful mama. You beautiful wife."

"And you, my dear man, are perfect. For me. I couldn't have imagined anyone better."

"You like?"

"You?"

"Being a mama."

"Yes."

"Do you like being a father?"

"Yes. Husband."

"Oh, you like being a husband too!" Samara laughed.

He leaned hungrily into her neck. "Time?"

"Not yet, but I guess I could please you in other ways…"

"Other ways?"

"Close your eyes."

Rake kept them open.

"Come on."

"No. Watch."

Samara put her hand under his shirt and ran her fingers along his waistband. She looked up at him and waited. He pulled her close, up against him. Yes, that was good. He liked that. She moved her fingers again, back and forth over the edge of his pants.

"Explode."

"Wait, my impatient man."

She undid the button.

He grunted and intertwined his hands in her hair.

She slid down and put her cheek on him, rubbed it, and after a minute looked up. He was flushed and serious, about to pounce. His breaths were long and deep. He held her head in both hands. "More."

She rubbed her cheek on him again. He was steaming up against her face. He started shaking, in spasms. He grabbed her hair. "Uhh."

"Rake! How? What? What was that? I'd barely gotten started."

"Sorry. You too delicious."

"Delicious. Hm," she said, but she was smiling. "Men!"

"What you mean men? Only me."

"Yes, only you."

"Only me sure?"

"Yes, I'm sure."

"Good," he said and dug his face in her neck. "So good."

Chapter 34

TWO YEARS PASSED, AND the baby grew. She was so beautiful with her tanzanite eyes and crème brûlée skin. She was magical, perfect, wild and smart. Oh so smart, her Gloria. She loved the church and the animals, especially Becks, their mutt, who accepted her pecks and prods and pulls without complaint. The brothers delighted in the child and spoiled her with love and any toy they could make with their knives and their hammers, always careful to not have protruding nails or sharp edges. Gloria was their baby, too, and they adored her. They sang and played handmade puzzles and taught the child to read, or rather, memorize, a few words they pointed to. She repeated everything they said and followed them around. Samara watched, always watched. From a distance, from nearby. She did not want to leave Gloria alone for one minute. Except with her father.

Rake had grown several more inches and became strong like an ox. His skin was browner from the sun, and his eyes glared blue like something from another world. They pierced her heart when he looked at her then at his daughter, nodding, absently touching the crucifix Guillaume had given him. He'd made one for her also and a tiny one for the child. She wore it on a chain around her neck. She wasn't sure, like Rake, but she liked it. She was grateful to these men who had saved them, given them a home.

Samara had moved her gun to her waistband, under her shirt. She cleaned it every day and sat at times, watching outside the window. Could she be imagining? She thought she heard the word "mama" a couple of times when everyone was sleeping and woke up startled. Rake got up to check each time, and there was nothing.

The brothers were boisterous in the evenings and laughed and played card games. It was good to hear them happy after what they'd been through. They enjoyed their homemade alcohol. They had a cellar now, in the basement. She thought she heard noises down there in the middle of the night sometimes, squeaking, the clanking of bottles. But there was nothing. She'd left the baby with Rake and offered the excuse of wanting to select a good wine for the following day and went downstairs to check. She searched everywhere, in every nook. Nothing.

She strolled down the mountain with the baby other days, just twenty yards, not too far, to scope out the area.

"I feel it," she said to Rake one afternoon. "Something is bothering me."

"A lot has happened in the last few years. Your mind is tired, you're tired. You have a baby to worry about. It's normal." Rake's speech had improved in leaps and bounds in the last three years since she'd known him. He'd learned to read and was even learning to write. He wrote her the same note every day. "Love mine."

And she loved him back. But her mind… Maybe she should just accept that everything was going well and nothing bad would happen. Maybe she should just enjoy being happy, well cared for.

She nestled into Rake that night after putting Gloria to sleep in the crib next to them.

She woke abruptly to barking and breaking, thuds and human groans, growling and whimpering. The sounds of destruction came faster and louder. She had her gun on the side table and reached for it. Rake jumped from bed and grabbed his knife from the sheath on the chair.

Samara was in her nightgown. No time to dress. She pulled on her shoes and went to the door. She opened it a crease and looked in the hallway. Empty. But the sounds of hell persisted. More breaking. She heard shouts of pain, a ballad of suffering.

"Wait here," said Rake.

"No, I'm coming." She glanced at Gloria, now awake and alert in her crib, closed the door, and went into the hall.

They walked together as quietly as they could to the dining room where much of the noise was now coming from. There was blood everywhere. More yelling could be heard in other parts of their home. She took off running, not saying a word to Rake. She was almost at the door of their room when she heard Rake holler in pain. She didn't turn back. She opened the door to their room and saw one of the creatures, bigger than she remembered. Now a gray man, bending over her daughter. She grabbed the gun from her back, pointed and fired—his brain blown to a million pieces. Smithereens. Chunks. All over her screaming child. She ran to get her, picked her up in one arm and walked. She went back to the kitchen where she found Rake on the floor, bleeding, knifing the leg of the man in front of him. Also gray. She shot him. Didn't even look at Rake. She moved from room to room. The scene was apocalyptic, blood covered the floor, her friends, hacked, their bodies desecrated. They had put up a good fight. Some of the grays were dead too. She kept going, room to room. Her baby on her hip. Her gun in hand. She could hear nothing. Not the crying, not the groans of those still battling. She pushed forward, next room, and another, and another. She blew them up. To pieces. To pieces. She could barely see in front of her. Go. Go. Keep going. Hold your baby. She heard silence. Nothing. She went around every room again, and the church, and the cellar. Her arm was locked around the child. Her face was full of human remnants. Splatters. Clumps. Her baby's head was full of blood. The rooms were now dead, all dead. She went back to the kitchen. Rake was lying on the floor, not moving.

She kneeled down and touched his forehead. He budged. The baby screamed. He was warm. "Come," she said. "I know."

She helped him up with one arm, held her daughter in the other. She took him to the room. There was blood on the walls, in the crib. She did not put the child down. Gloria kept screaming. Samara retrieved her sewing kit, a gift from Ignatius.

"I will be right back."

She went into the cellar and got a bottle of wine. She returned to their room and poured it over his wound. He groaned.

"You need to push it together as I sew."

She put the baby between her and Rake and threaded the needle.

She poured wine on one hand and the other and shook them till they were almost dry. "Take your hands and hold the wound together. I need to sew it or you will die."

"I can't," said Rake, and passed out. She positioned the baby between her knees, listening in case someone came. She looked out the window and back at Rake. She started to sew. She poured more wine over his cut. She'd have to find the moonshine they'd used during the birth. She knew they still had some. She'd seen Francisco sipping it for his throat.

She tore strips from a clean robe with her teeth and with one hand wrapped Rake's knife wound. She held the baby. She kissed him and took the child in the bathroom and washed her face and hair. The baby screamed. She washed her own face and hair and managed to change her clothes with one hand, switching the baby back and forth from arm to arm. She changed the baby's clothes. The baby screamed. She sat down and tried to console her. "It's okay. Mama has to look one more time and collect some things. We're going to go for a walk, far away from here. It's okay." She held the child and rocked her. She looked up at the ceiling. "Please."

The child finally fell asleep, in her arms.

She looked at Rake. How were they going to get out of here with him injured?

She put the child in the box with wheels and pushed with one hand, the gun in the other. She had slaughtered the whole bunch. The gray whatevers. The same ones from the beach, only— What had they been doing? Following her? Watching her? "Always trust your instinct," she mumbled to herself. What the f... She exhaled.

She was sad to see her friends dead but also angry. She went from room to room, did a full sweep of the building, picking up two machetes with one hand. Where was the dog? She put one under her arm and dropped the other. She checked under the sink for the moonshine. She found it in the pantry, at the very back. How would they go down that mountain. The dog wasn't barking. Where would they live? Surely there were more coming. Was it injured? They had to go away. Had it run off? The baby was crying. The doors were open. She whistled.

Samara left the second machete on the counter and took the alcohol in her hand. She pushed the baby to the room, went up to Rake and sat on the bed, and put the baby between her legs. The baby screamed. "Sorry sweetheart. Gloria, my good girl." The girl did not turn around. She kept screaming. Samara put the moonshine down and picked up the child. "Shh…it's okay. Papa is going to be okay.

Mama is here. Everything will be okay. It was just a bad dream." The child kept screaming.

She moved the child to her knees and used both hands to open the bottle. She lifted Rake's shirt and right over the bandages she poured the clear liquid. Rake grunted.

"Good. You're awake. How are you feeling?"

"Horrible. Are you okay? The baby?"

"She doesn't seem well. In shock, I think."

"The brothers?"

"Dead."

"All?"

"Yes. Can you walk? At least to the back. We have to hide until you can move further."

"I don't know."

"Just behind the greenhouse. At the canopy."

"I don't know."

"I will pack some milk for the baby and food and water for us. Can you hold her? Watch her?"

She thought better of it. What if he passed out again? And he wasn't strong enough to defend her if anything happened. "It's okay, get some rest."

Samara went with the baby in her arms and filled the box with whatever she could fit. She returned to the room and grabbed some blankets and put those inside too. She went into the supply room and found the rope. She looked around and packed everything and pushed with one hand. It was a mess. A bloody mess. It would start to smell soon.

She went back to the room. Gloria had stopped screaming and was sleeping over her shoulder, her thumb in her mouth.

"Are you ready? We have to— They might send more when their people don't return."

"Ready."

She gave him her free hand and pulled. He moaned and held his side. He ground his teeth and pushed himself up the rest of the way.

They walked slowly out behind the greenhouse. She left the supplies and went back to get them once Rake was safe outside. She kept the child with her.

She lay a blanket on the grass and put Gloria on it, careful not to wake her. She tied a string from the greenhouse to the tree behind it and pulled a blanket over and put down more blankets and pulled the baby box in.

Rake winced as he sat down.

She stayed up most of the night and listened. The baby slept in her arms and Rake slept like a corpse. She lowered her cheek over his mouth to feel his breathing a few times when he wasn't moving at all.

They would be okay. They would be okay. She checked the magazine of her gun. Empty. Nothing. She remembered the machete on the counter. Too late. There was no way she was going back in there.

They stayed two days. She cleaned Rake as best she could and checked his wound frequently. It didn't look infected.

"Do you think we could head down? How do you feel? We can take it slow. It won't be as hard as when we were coming up. It's downhill."

"The wagon," he said.

"The wagon?"

"Wagon in the shed. Our wagon. And take the goat. Attach it to the wagon."

She picked up her child, and with one hand fetched the wagon. She placed all their things in it and some in the baby box. She tied one to the other like a train.

"They will roll down," she said looking at them.

"Rope. A stake in the ground. Release."

"Okay."

Somehow they did it. With great difficulty. She had the baby on her hip. With her free hand she pushed a stake in the earth, attached to a long rope and the box and wagon in front. Full. She had to sit down on the ground with her baby and dig in her heels each time she gave the supplies a jerk to move past rocks or pebbles as they rolled down the hill. She followed, holding the rope, until the terrain was smooth and went back up to secure the stake. But she did it.

She had another rope attached to the goat, which was still up top. She set all the other animals free, made sure none of them were trapped when they left. She opened the chicken coop and pulled aside a now knocked-over fence. It was flimsy and moved easily.

They began to make the descent. She shook the rope and pulled lightly, and the goat followed. She did it again and again until it was alongside them. They paused at night, replenished their energy, ate, slept, hugged and in the mornings tackled the slope again.

Finally they were down on flat terrain. Rake was heaving and perspiring, but he had stopped bleeding.

"Are you okay? Do you want to rest a bit?"

"Tree. That tree over there."

They moved a few yards to the left and made camp in the shade. "Do you want some moonshine? I mean, to drink. Are you hurting?"

"No, I'm good, thanks."

"Come here, sweetheart." Gloria had not spoken a word all the way down, not a single mumble. Samara watched her as she got up and gazed at the roaming animals still around, several of which had run down the hill before them. The child raised her hand as if to touch them though they were many yards away.

"Gloria, come to papa."

"Sweetheart, come back." Gloria did not turn around. That was odd. She adored her mother and father. The sweetest little thing. The most beautiful girl in the world. "My baby girl, my love, my life, mama's good girl, come here. We can clap and sing a song."

Gloria kept wobbling towards a chick.

Samara got a funny feeling in the pit of her stomach. She walked behind her daughter and said, "Peekaboo." She did not react. Samara, alarmed, went in front of her. She kissed her on the cheek. "Do you want to get one of the chicks?" The child did not respond at all.

Samara pointed to the baby chicken. "Let's go get it." She walked the few steps and picked up a chick with one hand. "Look, nice chickie."

Gloria raised her hand and touched the little bird.

"Do you want to go show papa?"

She didn't answer or laugh or giggle and say papa like she normally would.

"I think I might have injured or traumatized her by bringing her with me to every room. She may have seen too much."

"Or the shots may have burst her ear drums," said Rake, pushing himself to a sitting position.

"I'm so sorry, sweetheart. So sorry. Mama is so sorry." She kissed the top of the child's head.

"We'll have to see. It's not your fault, Samara. There's nothing you could have done differently. I feel badly that I wasn't there to help you. He caught me off guard. He was hiding behind the door."

"You saved our lives by going out there. You know that, right? If you hadn't been there to delay him he would have come straight for us along with the other one in our room. I wouldn't have been able to take two at once. Thank you. You took a knifing for your daughter."

"And for my wife."

"Yes." Samara gathered her child, and the three of them sat together.

"Tomorrow," said Rake. "We can head out tomorrow. I can handle it."

Chapter 35

NOW THEY HAD A goat and a chick, the baby box, the wagon, herself, Rake and Gloria. They were conspicuous. And they could not walk fast. And Rake could not help her pull, and he could not yet hold Gloria.

She breathed deeply, took her baby in her arms. "Let's go, guys. We can do this. In the name… Oh, I almost prayed."

"Pray, Samara. Prayer always helps." What had happened to her barbarian of a husband? Three years is a short and a long time. He looked different, sounded different, but he was the same inside. She felt him. Except more.

"I sure wouldn't mind some help."

"In the name of the Father, the Son, and the Holy Spirit, thank you for giving us each other," said Rake.

"Amen!"

The girl didn't even look at them.

They walked and walked, and Samara pulled and pulled, away from all that wanted to partition them. They stopped and set up camp near sunset, and she let Gloria run around, within view. She chased the chick and tapped the goat. It was a good idea to bring them. They kept her entertained.

Rake made a ball out of cloth and rolled it to her as best he could. Every day he was healing and getting stronger.

"Where are we going, Rake?"

"Look for a house, somewhere, a safe house."

"Where? We can't go that way, there's Facticity. We can't go south, there's those crazy creepers that attacked us. We can't go north, there's the Commune. We can't go back to the church, and we can't go to that woman-hating place."

"Imogene," he said and winked.

"Yeah, right, so funny. She'd knock me to the moon if she saw me again. I stole you. You know, stole?"

Rake laughed, and winced in pain.

"I thought you said you were better."

"I am, but that was a hard laugh. Pretty funny. My little thief. Come here, my little thief."

"I would punch you if you weren't so hurt."

"Sure you would. Come here, love. I've missed you."

"You aren't serious, are you? How could you be thinking about that when you can barely walk?"

He shrugged. "A man's gotta eat."

She picked up the cloth ball and tossed it at him.

"Beasts!" she said and went to get her baby, stifling a smile.

Each day they walked, pulled, and watched. They had to stop and rest frequently. The water was running low. They had the goat, which helped, but it needed to drink, too.

They were heading north where it was cooler. The sun was burning her and the baby. Rake didn't seem as bothered. His skin was already baked by the sun. She was mesmerized each time she looked closely at him. And God made man, she thought.

"We have no weapons. Your gun is useless. You might as well leave it somewhere. It's just extra weight for nothing."

"I like it. The feeling of it. I'm keeping it."

"My killer. My woman. Who saved us. Boy, am I glad you have some skills."

"Nothing to be proud of, I assure you. You don't know all the evil I've done. Sometimes you have no choice. You need to become your environment in order to survive."

"I'm sorry you had to do all those things."

"Did you have to do anything bad to stay alive when you were alone?"

"I have not killed humans, no. I knew how to run, and hide well."

"How did your parents die? Do you remember?"

"It may be a false memory, because I was so young, but I found them both dead outside in the yard where they were working."

"That must have had an effect on you…"

"I don't know. You do what you need to do."

He looked upset and was breathing slowly, angrily. She thought she'd better stop the questioning, but the other times she'd asked she'd gotten barely anything. And she wanted to know him. To understand him better. The father of her child.

"I'm glad you haven't killed. But we don't have to talk about it anymore."

They walked until sundown and sat to have the last of their food and water.

"Rake, there's a pond, a big one, near the Commune. I fell in there. That's how I discovered there was a whole other world."

"You want us to go there?"

"What choice do we have? We need water, we need a hidden—I don't know, somewhere safe, or safe-ish."

"Do you want to go back?"

"I don't want to go without you, anywhere, but the baby…"

"Samara, I would come with you to the ends of the earth."

"They would turn you into a— I can't even say it."

"What?"

"A woman."

"A what!? For the love of God! I'm a man!" he said and clenched his hands and puffed up his chest.

"You are. You certainly are."

"That's not an option. Good Lord!"

"You could pretend."

"Samara, I am not a woman. I will not pretend to be a woman."

"Even if it meant being with us?"

"And will I have to do what you did?"

"Kill? Maybe. There are other jobs."

"Sounds like hell, Samara."

"Worse than the forcers? The woman burners? The breeder with over a hundred kids? The world is a horror, one thing worse than the next. What's so bad about the Commune when you think about it?"

He looked at her like he didn't know her. "Samara, please, the sun has gotten to your head. Do not talk like this anymore. We are staying and going to find a place where we can make a life."

"We have no way to defend ourselves. We are sitting ducks."

"Let's rest and tomorrow we are going to find a house."

In the morning they took off and walked north, towards water. Samara wasn't sure they were heading in the right direction, but Rake said he knew.

It was too hot. She and Rake had not drunk anything since yesterday. "Dig, Rake. Dig a hole for water. The baby needs water. The animals. And we do, too."

Rake dug ferociously in the dirt. "There is nothing here. Not near the surface anyway."

He wasn't looking all too well. "Let me see your cut. We should take the stitches out."

"It's fine."

"Are we going to the pond?"

"We are."

"Okay."

They slept holding each other, the child between them.

They woke still tired. They had no water and food. The baby whimpered. She took what she could from the goat, but there was hardly anything left. She gave it to the child.

Rake's lips were dried and cracked. He had been eating less and less each day so she and the child could have more. He looked thin. She lowered her head. She was tired. Just really tired. "Are we almost there?"

"Yes."

They walked like dead people. Samara put the child in the almost empty wagon and pulled. The goat fell, and they cooked her and picked the bones. There wasn't much meat. She had been too skinny. The chick had died a mile earlier. They buried it.

"Rake, I can't," she said falling to her knees, the wagon handle in her hand. "The baby doesn't look good." The child was quiet, her eyes big and protruding, and her skin was covered in red patches and blisters.

"Sit," he said, motioning to the wagon.

"No, no way. You'll die."

"I'm better. Sit."

She sat on the wagon holding her child, and Rake pulled them both. She did not know where he found the strength, but he found it.

Finally, she heard it. The sound of water falling.

"I hear it, Rake. I feel it. I feel it. There's moisture in the air. There's water nearby. She opened her swollen eyes as much as she could. I know this place. I know it. Go. Go. There."

She raised herself out of the wagon, placed her silent baby in it alone and grabbed the handle with Rake. Her small hand and his big hand, side by side. They pulled.

As they got closer he stopped, picked up the child and said, "Come." He held Samara with his free hand, and they walked to salvation.

It was glorious. A beautiful pool with a waterfall behind it. She walked right into the water and held out her arms. Rake passed the baby to her. She washed the child's head and face and put drops of water in her mouth. "Gloria, my girl. My beautiful. Come, baby girl. Come to mama." The child moved her head.

"Rake." She looked up. He was already in the pool, dunking his head backward, forward, bringing water up to his mouth.

Samara drank till her stomach felt like it would burst. She dropped more water into the baby's mouth. "Good girl, good girl, Gloria. Come to mama. Mama loves you. My good girl."

They found a shady spot, made a bed of leaves, and lay back for desperately needed rest.

"Food," said Rake after a while. "I will find food. We need food. I'll be back."

Samara sat by the edge of the pond holding her baby. She dropped more water over her mouth and washed the blisters. "You're such a good girl. Mama's girl."

The child moved her head but did not open her eyes.

"Oh God! God! God!" yelled Samara. She felt her eyes sting. What was this?! It was too much for her. "God!" she yelled again. She could think of nothing else to say. She bent over and cried. "God, oh God," she whimpered into the child. "God. God. God. Please." She too was limp. Done. She couldn't handle anymore. Too much. It was too much. Her baby. Her baby. Oh God, save her baby.

She sat there like that, crouched over, her lips on the baby's cheeks, tears streaming down her face, not saying another word. She felt a tug in her long hair. It was tangled in the child's hand. Another tug, and a moan. A cry.

"Oh, good Lord, my baby, my Gloria, my love, my beautiful child, my Gloria." And she wept. This time tears of gratitude. "Oh thank you, thank you. Thank you. My beautiful Gloria. My beloved child. My child. You are so beautiful." She kissed Gloria's cheek and sat her up gently in her lap.

"You're such a good girl. Such a good girl. Mama's here, and mama loves you. We will have food soon."

Rake had been gone a long time. She got up with the child and brought her in the water and got her to drink some more. They washed, and she held her and went back in the shade.

She needed food. They needed food. Where was Rake? She hoped he was okay.

She got up again and helped Gloria to walk around, small, slow, weak steps. But they were steps. She was alive. They were alive.

They waited three days and three nights. Rake never came back. She took the child in her arms, weak as she was, and walked around, digging through leaves and bushes. Ignatius had mentioned a path. She looked up. It was steep, almost a wall. She sat with the child on a rock at the bottom. She had to find it or they would die. She had no more strength to keep walking, and they were depleted.

On their last leg. They were dying. Where was it? Where had Clementine, her mother, if it was her mother, gone up? Where was the path? She had to find the way up. Think, think. She looked through more bushes and around trees, careful to not go too far from where Rake had left them. It had been days, and he had not returned.

She lay on the leaves with her child and dreamed of whistling. Whistling. Someone was whistling. A faint whistling.

Whistling. She opened her eyes and looked around and looked up where she thought she heard the sound coming from. She saw a human form and got up and waved with both arms. "Here! Here! We're down here! Help! We're down here! Here! Hello! Hello! Help!"

The person stopped whistling and looked around and then down at her. She picked up her child and yelled as loud as she could. "Hello! Hello!"

She waved again, slowly. They had disappeared. She sat down with the baby. What was she going to do? She waited and kept looking up, around, behind her. A while passed. She didn't know how long.

"Hey, I've been looking for you, figured you'd come back." The words were coming from the falls. She turned and saw Tony, wearing a dress, with lumps on his chest. He had long hair.

"Tony," she exhaled. "Help."

He held out his hand. "This way. Over here. This narrow strip of rock. It's slippery. Give me the child. Is she yours? Of course she's yours. She's lovely. Come."

"Yes, mine. No, I will hold her. Thank you."

She made her way over the strip and behind the running water. Tony followed her with his arms spread out. She was wobbly and kept stopping. She held her child, now alert and wide eyed, and let Tony help her climb the final steps. He put his arm over her shoulder, and they reached the top. She placed the child on the ground and held her hand.

"Thank you."

"No trouble. Are you okay? You don't look okay. Is Rake with you?"

"No," she said. She peered out past the cliff and scouted the area as far as she could. She saw nothing.

"Shall we go?" said Tony. "You look like death. And the child needs medical attention."

"Medical attention. Yes. One moment please."

She squinted into the distance. She saw a bunch of tiny moving shapes dragging something, and her heart fell. What was that? Was that her Rake? Had someone caught him?

She turned around and looked at Tony. "Thank you."

"Beautiful child. Congratulations."

"What should I do?"

"Say someone pushed you, and afterwards you were abducted."

They walked slowly towards town. There were civilians and guards rushing around. Some were stationed on lookouts. She could hear shots fired. Out of the corner of her eye she saw a woman sitting on a bench. She stopped walking and turned to look at her. She had short hair, a boy cut, and had on man's clothing. Time stuttered as their eyes met.

"We'd better get going," said Tony, "before we attract attention. You stand out, Samara. You've changed a lot."

"One minute, please."

She walked with her daughter toward the woman, slowly, peering at her. She knew her. The eyes. She knew them.

"Look what I had."

The woman gazed into her face and at the child.

"I'm a mama."

An army of soldiers had collected around her.

"Excuse me, but we will take the child now." The soldier nearest to her approached and reached for the toddler's hand. The child pulled away and held onto her.

"Wait," said Samara. She bent down and kissed her forehead and got up.

"She's damaged. She can't hear. Her uterus is no good."

The soldier picked her up, and the child screeched and stretched out her hands for her mother. He began to walk away.

"Her uterus is no good. Put that in her file."

Samara started to follow, but a soldier stopped her.

"Her uterus is no good!" she said louder. "Her uterus is no good!"

She pushed the man holding her and got out of his grip and went after the girl. "Her uterus is no good!" she shouted. They blocked her again. The guns pointed at her.

She fell to her knees and watched her screaming child taken away. She looked up at the soldier she had pushed, her face set like the dead. "Take mine."

Epilogue

My name is Samson. I live in the quarters with my comrades. We live in the Commune together. It is peaceful except when the rule-breakers break the rules. Then we have to discipline them. That is my job. I have a collection of rifles. Only the very best. I clean them every day. I listen to the shots in the distance like music to my ears.

When it's my turn I do a good job. I aim, and I fire. There is splatter on the ground. The cleaners come and take away the mess. I do not understand why they run. This is a good place. I do not understand why they jump. I watch them sometimes, one, two, three. Do not jump I told one the other day. Everything will be fine. Look at me. I'm fine. But they insist, and what can I do? I do not understand. I cannot fix what I do not understand.

It is my job to kill when I am on shift. After my shift I go to the bar. I play pool with the other guys there. It is not a jolly place. We look each other over to make sure each one of us is correct.

We take our cue stick and hit the balls. Sometimes I fantasize about ramming it down people's throats. I do not know why. I meet with a counselor each week to get to the bottom of it. She recommended electric treatments. They put nodes on my temples, and I feel a current go through me. I remember my name. My name is Samson. I remember I am a man. I cannot remember why I have scars. I cannot remember why I have a mark behind my left shoulder. I feel it melded in my skin. I do not know what it means.

I play pool. I eat. I sleep. I kill. I touch my scar, trying to remember what it means. Perhaps I should get it removed. Perhaps I should ask them to cut it off. Perhaps I should cut it off.

I walk around with my rifle some days, looking over the edge. I see people. Intruders. I do not know where they come from. Do they want to join us? Do they want to kill us?

Some days I see a brown man looking up. He does not move. He does not run when I raise my rifle and point. I am a good shot. I could get him. I do not know why I do not. He just stands there looking up. Not looking around. Just looking up at me, the killer.

I have short hair. It is meticulous. I brush it forty times a day. I brush it so much my scalp hurts. I walk around. I see a man sitting on a bench. The man looks at me. He is crying without moving. I do not know why he is crying. He looks at my gun. I raise it and aim it at him. He looks into my eyes and nods.

I walk around. I go to the edge. I see trees. What do they mean? I hear a sound. It is water. It cannot be. I do not see water. I see the brown man again. He is looking up. I do not know why I keep going to the edge. The man is always there now. I raise my gun. I am going to shoot him. I am going to kill him. Poof. A splatter. I do not do it.

I walk around. I go to my meetings. I get my shock. A child looks at me in the street. The child looks about six. It is a female. She has the bluest eyes. I look at her with a scowl. I do not want a child looking at me. I do not like them. My counselor tells me I do not like them. I raise my rifle and point it at the child. "Run," I say.

The child looks at me and does not run.

I walk around. I go back to the edge. I do not know why I am always going to the edge. Maybe I want to jump. Maybe I want to fly.

I walk around. I see the child again. She has scraped her knee. The other children are pushing her. She is crying. I look at her. I want to kill them. Kill them all. I do not know why I want to kill them.

I go to my counselor. Zap me harder. "I am having strange reflexes. Zap me till I feel nothing."

"But you remember nothing, Samson."

"That is true."

"If I electrify you more, you will be useless to us. You will be a vegetable and unable to fire your gun."

"Does the skin remember?"

"Remember what? What do you think you remember, Samson?"

"Nothing. I don't know what I am talking about. I remember nothing."

"That's good. If you were to start thinking you remember something or someone, you must tell us. Do you understand, Samson?"

"Who is there to remember?"

"There is no one to remember."

"I have a scar on my left shoulder, on the back of it. I do not know what it is."

"You were born with it. It is a birth defect."

"A birth defect."

"Correct. Are you having dreams? Unusual dreams."

"No."

"Thank you, Samson. It was a pleasure to meet with you today. Same time next week?"

"Yes."

I walk to my quarters. I take a shower. I do not look at my body. There is no mirror. There are no mirrors anywhere on the compound, and I am glad.

I change into civilian clothing. I am about to leave when I see something. It is yellow. It is the stuffing in my mattress. They have changed the mattress and made the stuffing yellow. I approach and put my finger in it. It is soft. It does not feel like mattress filling. I do not know what mattress filling feels like. I turn my finger. Something wraps around it. I take my knife and cut open a bigger hole. I pull and a thing comes out. It is a dress. A woman must have had this mattress before me. Why did she hide her dress in the mattress?

I cut up the dress into little pieces and go to the bathroom. I drop one piece inside the toilet and flush. I drop more and flush another and another. One piece at a time until they are all gone.

I walk to the bar. There is a knife in the wall with a shriveled thing under it. I do not know what it is.

The waiter says, "Hey, mate. What are you having?"

I am having beer. "What is that over there? The thing the knife is holding up."

"A salamander."

"Oh, okay. Thanks."

The waiter brings me the beer. It is cold. Refreshing.

I look at the thing on the wall. What is a salamander?

I do not want to play pool. I do not want to play anything. I am trying to remember what I cannot remember. Does a body remember? I cannot remember.

It is snowing outside. The people are walking by. They are huddled, the short men and the tall women. Nice. It must be nice to have someone. I wouldn't know.

I see the same child with the scraped knee. She is looking at me. The one the other children were beating up. She is passing by the window. She does not have a winter coat. She is looking inside the bar. The child is looking at me. In my eyes. I turn away. A tear falls on my cheek. I do not understand why. I wipe it as fast as I can. I do not want the other men to see. I look back at the window, and I cannot see the child. The window is fogged up. Someone has used their finger and drawn something on it. It is a symbol. A plus sign.

From the Author

I taught English for several years and quit to raise my children at home while designing books for independent authors, and simultaneously producing scripture coloring books.

My children have grown, and I am fulfilling my other lifelong dream, to write a novel. *All That My Skin Can Remember* broke me and elevated me and I will never forget the characters of Rake and Samara. And the beautiful Gloria, of course.

Thank you deeply, truly, for reading my book.

PS. The first versions of this page have been several times deleted as they were full of tears—of such gratitude. Dreams do come true.

Much love,

KR

Books by Kate Rang

All That My Skin Can Remember
Love in the Time of Apocalypse
I Saw You Under the New Testament Sky
(Coming Soon)